NINE-TO-FIVE
FANTASIES

Also by Alison Tyler

NINE-TO-FIVE
FANTASIES
TALES OF SEX ON THE JOB

EDITED BY
ALISON TYLER

Published in the United States by Cleis Press, Inc., 2246 Sixth Street, Berkeley, California 94710.

Printed in the United States.
Cover design: Scott Idleman/Blink
Cover photograph: iStockphoto
Text design: Frank Wiedemann

First Edition.
10 9 8 7 6 5 4 3 2 1

Trade paper ISBN: 978-1-62778-060-5
E-book ISBN: 978-1-62778-072-8

Opportunity is missed by most people because it is dressed in overalls and looks like work.
—Thomas A. Edison

Contents

INTRODUCTION:
THE "WANT" ADS

I possess a special talent—I can turn myself on by reading the newspaper. All I need to do is flip to the want ads and I'm gone, off to fantasyland, a faraway place filled with the workmen (and sometimes work*women*) of my dreams. I'll read: *Plumber Needed. Must have experience, tools...*

And I think, *Yes, I need a plumber, with an experienced tool.*

Or I'll read: *Opening for Chef. Seeking committed individual with a flair for food, a passion for cooking...*

And I envision fiery sex in the kitchen with a passionate chef.

To me, longing for practitioners of a specific profession is undeniably arousing. Have you always had a hard-on for a mechanic, gleaming with sweat, glistening with oil? Or a personal trainer, barking orders at you, making you obey? Or a pool boy...oh, dear lord, a pool boy. Life doesn't get much sweeter.

This book contains eighteen erotic fantasies about sexy occupations. Sure, what makes an occupation "sexy" is entirely up to each individual. But what makes a *story* erotic—well, after more than two decades in the industry, *that* is something I know about. The want ads may work well for inspiration, but they lack kink.

When I first dreamed up this collection, I imagined a book filled with my own fantasies. Not to be selfish, but I do know what revs my engine. I put out the call to authors everywhere: *Write me a story about fucking your favorite fantasy occupation.* I thought I knew what I would get back. However, I was thrilled to discover the variety that poured into my inbox: from cowboy to bookbinder, stage manager to IT guy, the authors in *Nine-to-Five Fantasies* pushed the boundaries on what makes for a sexy nine to five. Or six to twelve. Or eleven to seven.

Find your favorites in the table of contents and work from there. Forward, backward, upside down. There is no right way when fantasies are on the menu... (At least, that's what the delicious waiter told me.)

So what type of profession turns you on?

XXX,
Alison Tyler

GRIMY

Sommer Marsden

My mouth went dry when I saw him: tall and broad, dusty jeans and dirty plain white tee. His hard hat was red, not yellow, and the back had a TARDIS sticker on it. A geek construction worker? Was it possible?

I shook off the thought because there was nothing to guarantee that he had put that sticker on the hardhat.

His biceps flexed as he picked up the two orange cones that had resided in the hallway of my apartment building for weeks. Something to do with the stairwell and restructuring. Residents had been instructed to use the elevator or the stairs at the opposite end of the hallway instead.

My eyes fixed on the way his grimy shirt drew taut across his back when he moved, and it took me a minute to realize that he was now staring back. My key was in the door, my hand on the knob, my heart beating faster than it usually did when I took the stairs.

"Hi," he said.

I blinked and licked my lips. When he half-smiled I realized what I'd just done. My face heated with a blush, but I quickly sucked in a breath to get myself under control.

There was no way in hell this man could see into my head or know that I'd had a fixation on men like him my entire life. I'd never been to bed with a big, brawny construction worker because I'd never had the nerve—*gumption* my grandmother would have called it—to talk to one. Every time I was close enough to speak to one of these pillars of city life, I suddenly forgot how to talk.

This time was no different, so I nodded.

"Are you okay?"

My mouth felt like I'd swallowed a big spoonful of sand. Another nod from me, and he smiled.

"Okay then." He winked. It wasn't even smarmy or icky or anything. It was a wink that said we shared a secret. Or had a joke in common. Or just that he knew he was sort of pushing my buttons and liked it. But not in a cruel way, in an amused way.

He piled one cone on top of the other and hefted them up in one arm. That arm bore a tattoo of a crow caught in midflight.

Think of something clever to say. Ask about the sticker! Ask about the tattoo!

But I simply watched him walk away: nice ass in beat-up jeans with the bottoms of his pants legs sort of scrunched up around chunky, filthy work boots.

My pussy flexed just studying him.

Resigned to the fact that I was going to go into my apartment and get off with my vibrator to images of big, tall and studly going down on me, or even fucking me, I turned the key.

Then he called out. "Um, hello?"

I turned and realized I couldn't tell what color his eyes were.

His hair was brown. Not too long judging by what was peeking out from beneath his hard hat. It bothered me that I didn't know. And that thought bothered me because it was downright nuts.

I waited, watching him, still unable to speak. My heart was an erratic thing in my chest.

"You can use the steps now. In case you were wondering."

Then, wonder of wonders, I said, "Great," aloud. But my stomach dropped even as I said it because if we could use the steps that meant the work was done, which meant this stellar male specimen would be leaving and I wouldn't bump into him ever again.

He gave me a brisk nod and winked again. "Just so you know."

I tried to smile, hoping I didn't look crazy. But I was sure I actually did look crazy.

He sauntered off and I rushed into my apartment, slammed the door and rested against it.

"You are a moron, Lenore," I said aloud. Then I set about putting away my work bag, washing my hands and going to find that damn vibrator. I might have missed an opportunity, but I would be damned if I didn't use the meeting for fodder.

An orgasm was an orgasm.

I saw him the next day and started with surprise. My heart gave a kick in my chest. He was across the street doing work outside a building that was being renovated. Some god must have smiled on me because he looked up in time to see me. He grinned at me and it went right to my suddenly wet cunt.

I lost my mind then. Did something I never thought I'd ever have the nerve to do. I raised my hand and waved. Then a gust of wind came rushing up my wind tunnel of a street and lifted my skirt in a flirty bell around my thighs. I let out a cry and crushed my skirt to my legs, blushing all the while.

Then I turned tail and fled into my building, wondering if a person could actually drop dead of mortification.

It was barely five, I'd left work early and I was ready for a drink. A big fishbowl of a wineglass (a gift from my sister for my birthday) about half-full of merlot should do the trick. I was just pouring it when someone knocked.

Then my heart knocked crazily in empathy. Who the hell?

I suffered a brief but vivid porn-movie daydream where it was the studly construction worker come to show me the ways of a man who worked with his hands. He'd say something like, "I work wonders with wood—"

I snorted laughter, ripping myself out of the vivid mental vacation. Most likely it was Mrs. Stamos from two doors down asking if I'd seen Mr. Stamos. He often snuck up to the roof to smoke the cigarettes he was forbidden, but I never ratted him out.

I opened the door, already in the process of saying, "I have no idea where he is, Mrs. S—" but the words died on my lips.

"Studly," I blurted, and immediately prayed to choke on my tongue and die.

Because it was him. The big, dirty, hard-hat-wearing him, and when I said "studly" he chuckled so deeply and so perfectly my body wanted to shudder all over. When he grinned, it popped a single dimple in his right cheek and that just made me wonder what it would be like to stick my tongue into that dimple and taste the sweat on his skin.

"Hi," he said.

"Yes," I answered. It made no fucking sense.

He took off his hard hat and I saw perfect mink-colored hair. The color reminded me of gloves my father had worn in the winter when I was a little girl. An indescribable, supple brown.

His eyes, I saw, were icy, January-day blue.

"Yes?"

"Yes?" I said a bit louder. "What can I do for you?"

I pressed my thighs together to focus my mind and wished I hadn't. My body reacted as if he'd touched me then, my stomach quickening, my chest growing heavy, my pussy thrumming with blood and lust.

"I have a problem," he said.

My heart sank a bit. This was a good and proper business visit, nothing more, nothing less. I'd gotten myself worked up for nothing.

"What's that?" My voice was almost calm. Almost.

"Remember when we saw each other yesterday?" He took a step in, crowding me just a bit. I chewed my lower lip, tried to breathe.

"Yes."

"I can't stop thinking about you..." He blew out a laugh and ran a big dusty hand through that hair. Hair I found myself wanting to touch. "I don't even know your name. I'm David."

He stuck out his hand and I studied it. It was a nice hand. Dirty and nicked and I looked at it with no trouble imagining it on me. Holding me down, touching me, thick fingers sliding inside of me to fuck me.

"Lenore," I said, but it came out as more of a wheeze. I took his hand and just held it, letting him do all the work of shaking. I should have felt insanely embarrassed. Instead, I just felt sort of stunned.

"I hope you don't think I'm crazy?" He said it like a question.

I tugged him gently. His eyebrows went up, those chilly eyes flashing with humor. "No," I said. "I think I *am*, but not you."

I tugged just a bit more, and he was forced to choose. Pull

back from me, or move into my apartment. He chose the latter.

"So is it me or the profession?" he asked gruffly.

He was the one to shut the door. I was the one to thumb the lock.

"Yes," I said. "Both." Honesty is the best policy.

"'Cause lots of girls want to bang us hump busters," he grinned.

I nodded and just stared at him, pretty sure that I'd blink and come to sprawled on the sofa. He'd be gone and I'd be holding an empty bottle of wine and a remote. Having had a vivid dream, but just a dream.

Instead, I watched transfixed as he ran a finger up from my waistband to my chin. He tilted my face up to look at him and waited.

"I'm one. Of those girls," I said quickly. "But you...*you've* been in my head since..."

Tell him you got off three times thinking of him going down on you. Fucking you. Pinning you there and making you squirm...

My cheeks went so hot I touched them to see if they were red. They were on fire. He touched one then, too. "You're thinking really dirty things aren't you, Lenore?"

"Yes," I said. It was getting easier to talk because he wasn't laughing at me. He wasn't judging me. If anything, his fingers were moving through the air around me as if he wanted to touch me.

He walked forward, forcing me to walk back. My shoulder blades hit the foyer wall and he was right up in my face. Taller than me, wider than me, smelling of man and sunshine and dust. "Can I kiss you, Lenore?"

"Yes," I said. I'd have to pick a new word next time I spoke.

That thought melted away when he put his hands on my shoulders and braced me against the wall. His mouth was full and lush and when the heat of it touched mine I felt a small spasm deep inside. A faux orgasm. A little peek from my body at what an orgasm from this man might be like. I was less embarrassed than I might have expected to hear myself moan.

He made a gruff noise and held my upper arms, kissed me harder. His tongue snaked over mine, bullying me as I kissed him back. His grip on my arms felt like he could leave marks there. Vivid lines where his fingers had been. Simply imagining it had a rush of fluid slipping free of me.

"Oh fuck," I said.

He laughed softly. "I never thought I'd hear you say that. I never thought, at first, I'd hear you say *anything*."

"Would you like water?" I asked, stupidly. It was polite and ingrained in me.

"No."

"A soda?"

"No?"

"Oh god," I whispered, not believing I was going to say it. "Would you like me?"

"Yes," he said and kissed my neck. My nipples spiked, my stomach dropped. "I thought about you all night. The shy girl with the big, brown eyes."

I sighed as his fingers shoved up under my work blouse. His skin was warm against mine, and my skin rippled at the touch. He cupped my breast, peeled back the bra cup while shoving up my blouse and dipped his head to lick me. His tongue was searing and when his teeth found my sensitive skin, I jolted a little, gasped. I was so wet, so full and plump I just wanted him to fill me, but I didn't say anything. I was determined not to rush this.

"I should wash my hands," he whispered. "I'm a mess and I—"

"No please," I said. "No. Just stay as you are. Just..." I
dropped my head, that blush blazing in my face again.

"Just what?" he asked. "I just got you talking, don't stop
now."

"Touch me," I said quickly.

He pulled my blouse off over my head and my hair tumbled
wildly around my face until he pushed it back and kissed me
once more. The bra tumbled to our feet somewhere in that
moment. David nipped my lip and then my tongue and I ran my
hand along the front of his jeans to feel that he was just as far
gone as me. His hard cock pressed my palm, and I kissed him
harder.

"Take off this skirt," he said and then he flashed that half
grin and I admitted to myself I'd have jumped off the roof of the
building if he'd told me to and then flashed that smile.

He toed off his boots as he waited. The skirt hit the floor at
the same time his jeans did. My breath caught because when his
jeans dropped I saw he was bare underneath. His cock stood out,
thick and hard and blushing a lovely shade of reddish purple. I
started to drop to my knees to take him into my mouth, but he
beat me to the punch.

David's knees hit the floor with a muffled thud and he pressed
his face against my stupid work panty hose. The kind that were
not sexy or fetching. The kind that had a big seam that ran
from the crotch to the waistband. But he didn't seem to care.
He pressed his face to the front of me and his breath heated
my pussy in an entirely foreign and utterly spectacular way. He
nudged my clit through the hose and the panties with his rigid
tongue.

I couldn't help myself. I drove my fingers into his thick hair
and tugged a little. I ground my pussy to his mouth and wished
upon a million stars that the fabric would simply disappear. But

that didn't happen. What did happen was David grabbed the sides of my hose and panties combined and yanked. With the two bunched up around my knees, I was unable to spread my legs. So when he buried his face between my thighs and started to lick me with gentle but brutal laps of his tongue, the friction was almost unbearable.

"Jesus," I sighed. My mouth was moving now. Spilling out words I hadn't intended to say and he was just eating me out, licking me so I was slick and shivering, until he took one of his thick workingman fingers and shoved it into my pussy, pressing my G-spot expertly.

I came. Back pressed to the cool white wall, my hose binding my knees together, my hair hanging in my face. I was sure anyone in the hall could hear me because I wasn't being quiet. Not at all.

"Hurry, hurry," I said.

"Hurry for what?" He chuckled again. I loved the sound of his laugh. It was molasses drizzling over warm pancakes.

"I want you to fuck me, that's for what," I blurted, trying to push my hose down so I could move.

When I said it so matter of factly, he grunted, his eyes darkening.

His cock twitched and I took my turn now, dropping to my knees, sliding my lips along his shaft, licking greedily at the crown to taste the sweet bite of precome on my tongue.

If I hadn't known better, I'd have thought I was hurting him. But one of his big hands settled on top of my head and the other cupped the back. He anchored me, thrusting fluidly forward without gagging me or going too fast.

I sucked a deep breath in through my nose. Relaxed my throat. Took him down as I relished the thought that this was happening. Finally happening! It almost seemed surreal but there he was when I touched his thighs, his skin under my fingertips, his cock thrust deep in my throat.

"Stop, stop," he grunted with a strangled laugh. David pushed me back onto the foyer carpet and ran his hands over my belly, the tops of my thighs. The thought of those hands, busted up from work, coated with grime from dusty construction, now skimming my skin, had me panting.

I put my arms around his neck and pulled him in, kissing him. I swirled my tongue over his and trembled when he nipped my tongue. When I gasped, his teeth found the fragile skin of my clavicle and nipped me there.

"Spread your legs for me, Lenore," he said.

The way he said my name—a name I often hated—had me on the verge of coming.

I did as ordered and he pulled back for a moment, finding his pants, his wallet, a condom. The snap and scent of latex filled my head, and then he was running the tip of his cock along my soaking wet slit.

I arched up, trying to hurry him along.

He tsked me good naturedly. "Patience."

If you had any idea how long I've waited...

Instead I said, "I am patient. Mostly..."

He slid into me with one sleek thrust, surprising me and stealing my breath. Then he stilled, staring down into my eyes as he filled me but didn't move.

My pulse pounded in my throat and head. My heart hammered my chest and the tom-tom beat of it filled my belly and cunt too. I groaned and gripped his thick forearms with trembling fingers.

"Please, move. Please!"

So he did. Giving me that half smile again that reminded me of the King of Rock and Roll, of course. But somehow it was a bit more rakish. A bit more dangerous on his pretty, pretty face.

I wrapped my legs around his waist, opening my body to his, and it was his turn to groan. His forearms shook as he lowered down to kiss me again. "You're a challenge, Lenore."

"I am?"

"You make me want to just let go."

"Funny, I know that feeling."

I knew it was bizarre, but for once I was going to take a situation at face value.

When I drove my body up to meet his thrusts, his face seemed to change with the pleasure. Becoming more feline, his cheekbones more chiseled.

"Hands up," he said, and then he made a low sound when I readily obeyed.

He clasped them above my head with his strong hands and ground his hips back and forth, back and forth before thrusting deep over and over again. He watched me closely and when I came, he kissed me quiet.

My pussy filled with one sweet flutter after another.

"Turn over for me," he said.

His hands caught up in my hair as I went. Wound it tight, used it as a lead. It made my skin prickle with arousal the way he manhandled me. That was what I wanted. To be handled. Touched. Told and taken.

He spread my legs to his liking, found my slit again and drove into me, using my hair as a rein. I cried out as he hit my G-spot without mercy and when I came a third time, he let my hair tumble loose around my face, grabbed my hips and thrust deep and hard until he was crying out harshly.

Outside something boomed and the building rattled a bit. "Ahhh, shit," he laughed. But he hadn't moved, and his palm was smoothing over the swell of my asscheek. His calluses rasped on my skin, and I pushed myself back into the palm of his hand.

I thought I could have stayed there all damn night if he kept touching me that way. Fantasy fulfilled, I thought. But now...oh now, I wanted more.

"I guess I should go," he said, finally pulling free.

"I...oh..." I'll admit it. My heart sank. But this was just a onetime thing. A fling. A quickie. A steamy fuck with a stranger. Something to cross off my bucket list... He interrupted my internal pity party to say, "I'm not even supposed to be gone. I took a quick break to 'get coffee,'" he said, making air quotes.

"Oh..."

He stood, pulled off the condom and put it in the trash when I pointed the way. Watching him walk bare-assed was a plea-sure I wouldn't soon forget. Then he yanked on his jeans and leaned in to kiss me. "Can I come back later tonight? Maybe be a proper gentleman? Bring some wine? A pizza?" He looked down at himself. "Maybe not be so dirty."

I smiled, everything in me lifting up a little and soaring. "I'd be curious to see you not dirty." It might be more than once, after all.

"Same goes for me, Lenore."

I raised an eyebrow. "I don't understand."

"I'd like to see you *not* dirty. You were pretty dirty just now."

I gaped at him and he smiled. "Just kidding. But I did actu-ally like how dirty you were." He touched me once, touched me twice. "Shy girl with the big, brown eyes," he said, winking, and then like a shot he was out the door.

I shut the door softly. I'd finally done it. And the best part was, he'd be back and I'd probably—hopefully—get to do it again. And I'd remember to ask him about that sticker on his hard hat.

BONANZED

Kate Pearce

The dude ranch wasn't quite how I'd pictured it. Sure, there were cowboys and horses, and a big barn, and all that stuff, but it was no *Bonanza*. I'd grown up on TV cowboys and booked this vacation to get up close and personal with them—if you know what I mean. I'd obviously forgotten the whole *ranch* part and focused too much on the *dude,* because there were horses and rides and cookouts.

By day two, I was exhausted in a healthy outdoor kind of way, and eating like a horse as well as riding one. When my name was called to mount up, I couldn't get my foot high enough to reach the stirrup. One of the ranch hands, a cowboy called Chase, came over and offered me a boost into the saddle. He had big square hands. I liked the way his fingers curled around my knee as he settled my foot into the stirrup. I flexed my muscles and pointed my booted toe, aware of his longest finger inching up the seam of my jeans.

"Is that better?"

He wasn't much of a talker, but I was okay with that. "Thanks."

I couldn't see his face, only the top of his Stetson. His fingers tightened for a brief moment around my upper thigh and then let go. I almost came in my jeans.

"I don't suppose you give private lessons, do you?"

"It depends."

"On what?"

He looked up at me, his narrowed blue eyes the same sun-washed color as the hazy morning sky. His skin was tanned, his mouth lush and his lower lip full.

"On what you're willing to learn."

"How about you meet me in the barn after dinner and explain your strengths?"

"And miss the s'mores around the campfire?"

Was he laughing at me? But, god, I did love s'mores, almost as much as I did cowboys... "After that then."

"Sure." He patted my horse's butt and sent me on my way.

The s'mores were good, the communal singing god-awful. He caught my eye over the flickering fire and nodded toward the barn. I pretended to yawn, stood up, smoothed down my denim skirt and smiled at the nearest campers.

"'Night everyone. All this fresh air is killing me!"

Everyone laughed, and I strolled away, taking a more circuitous route back to the barn and coming in through the other side. A big blackboard with all our names and the names of our horses took up most of the wall. The lighting was dim. I could hear the occasional snort and clatter of a shoed hoof on the cement floor. I inhaled the intoxicating scents of hay and leather, and smiled.

"Ms. Pattison."

He was over by the tack room, one shoulder propped against

the door frame. I couldn't quite see his expression, but I hoped it was as anticipatory as mine.

"Mr. Chase."

He smiled. "Chase will do just fine. What can I do for you?"

I strolled over to him and placed my hand flat on the front of his denim shirt. Close up, he smelled of marshmallow, chocolate and the smoke from the fire. I wanted to strip him naked and lick the flavors off him, one by one.

"It's Denise and you can do anything you want to me."

He caught my wrists and drew my hands behind my back.

"Anything?"

He made it more of a statement than a question, his gaze assessing, and his hands firm on my skin. He yanked me closer until we were pressed together from knee to shoulder, breast to chest, cunt to cock. I rolled my hips against the hard rod of his erection, and his hand clamped down on my ass.

"Hold on."

He picked me up, shutting the door with the heel of his boot, and dumped me on a stack of hay bales. I stayed put while he locked the door and then turned back to me, his smile predatory. The faint sounds of "Kumbaya" filtered through the ill-fitting wall planks. He took off his gloves and flexed his fingers, his gaze on my crotch. Helpfully, I eased one knee to the side and drew my booted foot up.

"Do you like what you see, cowboy?"

"Better if you lift up your skirt."

I complied and his breathing hitched as I displayed my bare, shaved sex. Just to make sure he was paying attention I swirled my finger around my clit.

"Look, I'm already wet."

"Must be all that singing." He came closer and sucked my

finger into his mouth. "Mmm...and you're all creamy like the s'mores."

He went down on his knees, and this time I was the one who was holding my breath as his tongue came out and licked a slow lascivious path from my clit to my ass. Two broad fingers penetrated my cunt, and I moaned.

He looked up at me. "Is this what you want, lady? A quick fuck?"

"Well, not the quick part."

"It's going to have to be. I have to get back and round up the happy campers and make sure the fire is out." His thumb circled my clit and pressed hard and I came just like that. He eased a condom out of his jeans pocket.

"Would you like to put that on my dick?"

"I'd love to, but not quite yet."

He grimaced as I tried to unbutton his fly, the thick wedge of his cock making it difficult. I hummed in anticipation as his shaft was revealed inch by slow tantalizing inch.

I leaned in and sucked the crown into my mouth, enjoying the taste of leather and man and precome swirling over my tongue. His hand slid into my hair urging me on. I drew him deeper and sucked harder.

He groaned and his hips rolled as he fucked my mouth, taking control away from me.

I pulled back and looked up at him. "Quickly, then, cowboy."

He grinned, one hand already wrapped around his cock as he expertly covered himself. "Yes, ma'am."

And then he was shoving himself inside me and I was wrapping my legs around his pumping hips and we were coming and coming and...my ass was being poked by straw. I surged away from the pricking sensation and impaled myself on *his* prick instead, forcing another climax and a corresponding grunt from my compliant partner.

We disentangled ourselves and he cleaned up, tossing the condom into the trash and buttoning his jeans. I stayed where I was, skirt rucked up, legs splayed wide, my nicely throbbing cunt exposed to the cool night air.

He gave me a regretful glance. "I really do have to go."

I licked my well-kissed lips and thought about his cock. "I'm leaving tomorrow afternoon."

He unlocked the door. "I know."

"So this is my last night."

He sighed and turned back to face me. "I'll fuck you as much as you like after I've settled everyone in." He hesitated, his gaze on my mouth. "Hell, you can come back to the bunkhouse, there are four of us in there."

I sat up.

"*Four* of you?" I pretended to swoon. "Sounds like heaven to a *Bonanza* groupie like me."

"We call them buckle bunnies these days." His slow smile was catching. "Jeez, you sure do like your cowboys, don't you?"

I smoothed down my skirt and offered him my hand. "Yes, sir, I sure do." He helped me down and I grinned up at him. "There aren't many in Manhattan, so I have to stockpile when I get the opportunity."

O FOR EFFORT

Delilah Night

I'd picked mind-blowing sex with Paul over studying one time too many. *See me* had been written in lieu of a grade on the last page of my midterm. My hand shook as I raised it to knock on Professor Kumar's door.

Professor K's was the last class I wanted to fuck up. I'd worked so hard to get noticed. Until this semester I'd been a diligent student who went above and beyond on assignments. I could always be counted on to add value to the class discussions. I'd been on the road to a personal recommendation for Yale's history PhD program.

That Professor Kumar was brilliant, gorgeous and British only motivated me further. My Anglophilia was such that he could've read the phone book up at the lectern, and I still would've paid rapt attention. However, he visibly burned with a passion for history. He paced as his voice rose and fell, showcasing his fierce intellect and tight denim-clad ass. He wasn't afraid to crack a joke—usually relating to a Brit teaching American history.

Lecture days often ended with my panties soaked. I'd miss the first fifteen minutes of my calculus class because I had to escape to the women's room to relieve my aching clit. By my second course with him, I knew better than to schedule anything after class. My post-class routine that semester: back to my dorm room, lock the door, strip, grab a vibrator.

On my knees in the lectern, sucking his cock while he lectured. Getting fingered in my research library cubicle. A spanking. Helplessly tied to my dorm bed. Ripping one of the endless parade of white Oxford shirts off his body. Him, licking my cunt. In the exhibit he'd organized a trip to, our mating reflected in the silver creations of Paul Revere. What he'd do to me under the pretense of "helping" me during office hours—over, under, on top of his desk, in his chair, up against the door, the bookcases, the window.

I'd burned out the motors in four vibrators by the end of the semester.

When none of his classes fit my schedule or my requirements junior year, I'd joined history club to get a monthly fix of my favorite eye and ear candy. It hadn't been enough.

The Indian soccer player one floor below me had been the recipient of my pent-up lust on several occasions.

I "accidentally" dropped my towel in front of him in the coed bathroom.

"Like what you see?" I'd asked.

He nodded.

"Would you like to see me on my knees?"

He nodded again.

I led him to the shower stall and sank to my knees, focusing on his cock, worshipping it the way I wanted to worship Dr. K's.

A British banker I'd met in a bar had also been an attempt to satisfy my fantasies.

Just fuck me from behind. I love it doggy-style. Talk to me while you fuck me.

Both had been fun, but neither slaked my lust for Dr. K.

"Ms. Cohen," Professor Kumar said, as he gestured for me to enter and take a seat. "I asked you here to discuss the dip in quality of your work. Is there anything I should know?"

"I should've asked for an extension. I got behind, and I left it until the last minute. I'm sorry," I babbled.

Professor Kumar leaned back in his chair, fingers steepled. "This is your third class with me. You're aware of my no-extensions policy. You've been an exemplary student. So what could keep a diligent young woman such as yourself so busy that you skived off on the assignment?"

"The sex," I confessed, and immediately blushed.

"The sex, Ms. Cohen? You have my attention. Please, continue." His eyes took a slow inventory of my body as if he'd never noticed that I was a woman before. His gaze lingered at my breasts. I had skipped a bra today, when it became clear that laundry had also taken a backseat to Paul's touch. My nipples hardened, impudently thrusting against the all-too-thin fabric of my T-shirt. I shifted in my seat, clenching my thighs together under my skirt as my clit swelled. I felt myself slicken between his unrelenting inspection of my body and my memories of the sex.

"It's been really intense," I whispered. "I've never had such powerful orgasms in my life—"

"Let's see how many times you can come in an hour," Paul had said as he raised an eyebrow at me in challenge two nights ago. *"In two? In four?"*

First I'd moaned for more. Then I'd begged to be fucked. I hadn't expected that he'd hold a vibrator to my clit as he did so. He would let me rest, to allow my system to start to calm. Then his hands, his mouth, or a toy would find me again. It was something of a miracle I was capable of walking yesterday, much less finishing a term paper.

"Your excuse for not writing your paper in a timely fashion is that you were busy having too many orgasms?"

I lost the ability to speak as Professor Kumar put a hand on my knee. He raised an eyebrow as if to say, *Your move, Ms. Cohen.* I nodded assent to both the spoken and unspoken questions. Slow and deliberate, Professor K's hand began to journey up my thigh. My skirt slid higher as I spread my legs to provide him access. He cupped me, thumb stroking me through my increasingly wet panties.

"Yes," I managed. "Please. Yes."

The chance to make real years of fantasizing? HELL YES.

My pulse sped as Professor Kumar's finger slipped beneath the fabric to my aching clit.

He leaned in, breath hot against my ear, and murmured, "If your problem was too many orgasms, perhaps you should demonstrate some self-control? You mustn't orgasm until I give you permission. If you can manage that, we'll discuss your options. Are you up for it, Ms. Cohen?" His thumb made lazy circles on my clit as he propositioned me.

"God, yes," I moaned, as I rocked against him.

Professor K sat back and smirked when my eyes flew open at the absence of his hand. "Give me your knickers," he commanded, holding out a hand.

I surrendered the floral cotton eagerly.

He pulled me into his lap, my back pressed against his chest. His lips and teeth worked magic on my neck. Professor Kumar's hands were busy under my shirt, tugging, rolling and teasing the nipples that had made themselves known to him not five minutes ago. My head fell back against his shoulder. My hips gyrated, craving his hardness in approval.

Was the office door locked? Did I care?

"Little slut. Wet and open for me. Desperate for me to bend you over the desk and roger you? Where would you like it—your quim or your arse?" he growled.

The mental image evoked caused me to gasp. "I've never..."

"Never taken a cock up your arse?" My professor positioned my cheeks over a suddenly hard cock. His teeth grazed my neck as fingers plunged into my cunt, and began to fuck me. The world telescoped down to his touch, and my building need. "Does the idea turn you on?"

Paul, sliding a finger into my last bastion of virginity. "What do you think?"

"I-I don't know," I stammered.

"I'm scared. It's so tight, and..." I'd shaken my head no. I was surprised then, that when Paul had removed his finger, I'd craved its return.

Professor Kumar's fingers returned to my clit. "Liar."

I shuddered. "I like the idea," I confessed. "Please, I'm so close."

"Come without permission and you'll fail the paper, and my class. Midterms are worth forty percent of the grade, Ms. Cohen," he warned me, fingers tapping a rapid beat on my clit and pushing me ever closer to release and failure.

"Please! Please, let me come!" I pleaded.

"No. Why not let me fuck you in the arse? I might let you come then," he suggested.

The temptation of orgasm warred with fear of the unknown.

What is it with men and the ass?

I'd go crazy if I didn't come. Need overwhelmed me.

"Yes," I whispered.

"That's my little hussy. Get naked and bend over my desk," he ordered, releasing me.

Deprived of his touch, my body felt hollow. I yanked off my clothes, uncaring where they landed. The wood of the desk was cool against my hips. My breasts took up several days in March as I leaned over his calendar. The scent of leather tickled my nose as I lay my head next to his grade book.

Paul's hand, encased in leather, spanking me. Sucking his leather-encased finger as he slid inside me, his hips mimicking the enthusiasm of my mouth, turning me wanton.

Professor Kumar's hands rubbed my asscheeks. He dipped a finger into my dripping pussy, spreading the slickness upward and back.

He caught me trying to squeeze my thighs together, trying to relieve the ache. "Stop squirming. You'll get your pleasure when and if I say, not before," he ordered, moving my feet wider apart. Cool air tormented my aching cunt as he stepped away.

I heard the sharp metallic zing of his jeans opening, the rustle of material, and finally the tear of a foil packet.

His cock. I want to see it.

A reproving slap landed on my ass. "Naughty little tart. Trying to get a look, were you?"

"Please," I begged softly.

"No." One hand pushed me back against the desk.

Another flurry of spankings. I moaned and raised my hips, silently asking for more.

"Dirty. Girl. Ask. For. It." Each word was punctuated with a smack.

"Spank me. Fuck me. Use me," I whispered.

"What was that, Ms. Cohen?" My ass began to burn as the slaps increased in intensity.

"Please, spank me. Use me. Fuck me. Please, please fuck me," I pleaded.

"Have the courage of your convictions, Ms. Cohen. I don't

believe you at the moment. Perhaps you just want a spanking for your lazy work, and to take the consequences of your extra-curricular activity?" He was hitting my sweet spot with every smack. Each time his hand connected, I felt the impact all the way from my cheeks to my clit.

"Fuck me. Please, fuck me," I chanted, uncaring if anyone heard me.

The department head could walk in and I'd still beg for more.

In one glorious stroke, his cock filled my cunt. I placed one knee on the desk allowing him deeper inside. Professor K cupped a breast, squeezing it. I sighed with pleasure as his fingers began rolling and tugging at the nipple.

"So good," I moaned.

His fingers bit down cruelly. An electric jolt screamed from my nipple directly to my clit.

"More," I begged.

I'd never considered my nipples particularly sensitive before Paul.

"That's because no one's taken the time to train them," Paul told me.

He produced a set of nipple clamps from a drawer. Fear and desire had hardened my nipples for him without so much as a touch. When the cold metal had bitten down, I'd first cried out in pain. Then Paul had leaned forward and licked the pinched skin, pleasure taking control again.

Professor K's thrusts began to speed up. My vision began to blur as my body tightened. Then, just as fast as he'd entered, he withdrew. I cried out, begging for his return.

No! So close!

A finger pulsed against my asshole, teasing the opening.

"Tell me what I want to hear," he growled. "If you ever want to orgasm, or have a prayer of a passing grade, tell me to fuck to you in the arse."

I was going to try it anyway. If this is how I can have him, yes. Yes.

"Do it. Fuck me in the ass," I moaned in capitulation.

Professor Kumar traced the slick path from my cunt to my ass over and over, spreading my wetness to lubricate me. His hand tormented my clit, keeping me aroused and dancing at orgasm's edge. Pressure became a burning sensation as the head of his cock opened my virgin hole. I felt like I was being split in two and I started to pull away, scared.

"Shhh…just a moment more, darling," the professor crooned.

Like magic, once the head had fully entered me the pain was gone. His shaft slid home. He stilled, balls brushing the tops of my thighs.

"There you go. Good girl," he murmured, his finger again teasing my clit. "Tell me how it feels."

"I'm good. It's good. But my cunt feels so empty. Hungry—" I panted as I neared the edge yet again.

He laughed. "That's because you're a proper little slut. Want something up your cunny and your arse at the same time do you?" He began to rock against me.

Riding a cock. One up my ass.

"And one in my mouth," I moaned.

"What a picture you'd make," he growled. He fucked my ass in earnest now, sliding back and then slamming deep. His balls slapped my thighs as he thrust.

"Come for me," he whispered.

I surrendered to the cresting pleasure. My body tensed. Professor Kumar's hips pumped, fingers relentlessly working on my already overworked clit. A flash of heat spread. The pulse at my throat boiled. My vision blurred. Then a tsunami of an orgasm hit me and dragged me under. A hand covered my mouth, muffling my sobs of pleasure. I was glad of the desk when my legs gave out.

Seconds, minutes or hours later, I heard the Professor grunt. His weight fell against me. "Well done," he murmured.

That was amazing. Why did I wait so long to try it?

Professor Kumar slid out of me. My ass felt sore, stretched and well used. I wasn't going to be able to sit without remembering this for at least a day or two.

"I don't think I can move," I whispered. "I can't even feel my nose."

He chuckled. "By the by, your essay actually earned a B-plus."

"Paul, *you bastard*. You said we had to keep school and our relationship separate. I thought I'd actually—" My head fell back on the desk as relief and irritation warred with each other.

Unrepentant, Paul chuckled, and squeezed a sore cheek. "You told me that you'd fantasized about this, Abby. Don't get your knickers in a twist. Now, get dressed or we'll both be late to seminar."

I gathered my clothes. "I need my panties, Paul."

An evil grin flickered as he tucked them into the pocket of his jeans. "No you don't."

DRIVER'S SEAT

Sophia Valenti

D an and I made the rounds of the raucous backyard gathering that was our wedding reception, thanking our friends for sharing the day with us. The sun had already set, the inky sky matching the hue of my midnight-blue, velvet-flocked gown, but countless hanging lanterns illuminated the cheerful crowd. They seemed fully intent on continuing the celebration long after we'd taken our leave of them.

My friend Louisa had insisted on holding the festivities at her recently renovated Victorian home. It was a stunning backdrop for photos of our steampunk-inspired wedding party, who were attired in colorful waistcoats and corseted dresses.

I saved my last good-bye for our hostess, who rushed toward me with arms outstretched, and lace-trimmed bell sleeves billowing, to give me an exuberant hug.

"Congratulations, my love," she said before kissing me on the cheek. She rested her hands on my cinched waist and looked me in the eye as she said, "The limo's waiting at the front of the house."

"Lou, I told you we don't need a driver!"

"Yes, yes, you do," she answered with a smirk. "It's my gift to you," she added with an emphatic nod of her head. Without another word, she turned toward my new husband, light glinting off of the polished brass goggles that sat atop her ginger hair, and Dan embraced her in a bear hug that caused her to rise up on the toes of her butterfly-festooned boots.

I couldn't fathom why Louisa would care how we made it from her house to the bed and breakfast in town—especially since our own car was parked in the driveway, but I didn't try to argue with her.

As we took our leave, Dan held my hand and helped me navigate the dark, grassy path from the yard to the house; my crinolines rustled noisily with every careful step I took. A large, vintage car soon appeared in our view, silhouetted by the full moon.

"A limo, huh?" Dan said, with a chuckle.

"Yeah, why we'd need one for a fifteen-minute ride..."

"I know." Dan squeezed my hand. "She's just trying to be nice. Relax and enjoy it."

As we approached, a small, trim figure emerged from behind the car, triggering the motion-sensor lights at the front of Louisa's home. We could now clearly see the vintage black Rolls-Royce, its door being held open by a petite blonde, whose short platinum hair was slicked back beneath her black chauffeur's cap. Her formfitting white shirt and black leather underbust corset enhanced her subtle curves, and her skintight black leggings were tucked into shiny patent-leather boots, giving her a sleek, streamlined appearance. This woman was definitely built for speed.

"Good evening," she said, the words falling from her lips in a lazy drawl. She unabashedly allowed her gaze to travel from my elegant updo to my buttoned-up ankle boots. Despite her supposed role as our driver, I didn't think for one minute that she was there to serve me. The look in her eyes seemed absolutely predatory, and it sparked an unexpected flare of arousal inside me. With one hip cocked, she leaned against the car door, letting a fingertip casually trace the bottom of her glossy pout.

"Uh, Bridget," Dan began nervously, not tearing his eyes away from her. "You guys know each other?"

"No." I looked at Dan, who seemed as flustered as I was.

"Ah, but we have all night to correct that," she responded, the boldness of her response surprising me and thrilling me all at once. "Come on in," she said, gesturing toward the car's interior. "I'm Liza. I'll take you where you need to go."

I dimly recalled Louisa telling me about a friend of hers who worked as a chauffeur because of her love of classic cars. Suddenly, all of the details snapped to the forefront of my mind. Liza. Her kinky friend Liza. The one who also had admired photos of me and Dan that hung on the walls of Louisa's home. At that moment, I knew our time with Liza didn't have to be fifteen minutes. It could be so much more.

Once Dan and I were safely inside the car, Liza slammed the door shut and took her time coming around to the front seat. It was almost like she knew we needed a few minutes to ourselves.

"What do you think of Liza?" I asked in a hushed whisper, taking Dan's hand in mine. He and I had previously enjoyed threeways, but I didn't know how he'd feel about sharing our wedding night with a stranger—albeit a beautiful one with a penchant for kink.

I saw hesitation flash across his handsome face, almost as if he was wondering if my question was a test, but he quickly gathered his wits.

"She's stunning," he answered, his voice filled with raw honesty and lust.

Before I could say another word, Liza opened her door and slid into the front seat. But that was no matter. Dan had given me all the answer I needed, and I gave his hand a reassuring squeeze. Liza adjusted her rearview mirror, the reflection of her green eyes meeting mine. She held my gaze for a long moment, letting the heat between us build, before she gripped the tip of her cap between her thumb and forefinger, giving me a nod and a wink. Then she turned the key in the ignition and steered the car toward the main road.

My heart was pounding beneath my tightly laced corset. I'd been looking forward to our wedding night, but now that such an intensely erotic possibility was being dangled in front of me, I could barely contain my excitement.

Liza didn't speak during the short drive to our destination, but she did continue to steal smoldering glances at me in the rearview mirror whenever she could. Each time our eyes met, I felt another wave of desire course through me. I snuggled closer to Dan, who whispered, "You want to play with her, don't you?" I merely nodded in response, and he laughed, a low throaty chuckle that betrayed his arousal.

Let me tell you, fifteen minutes pass by quickly when you're holding your new husband's hand and trying to decide on the best pickup line to lure a hot blonde into your honeymoon suite. But as it turned out, I shouldn't have fretted one bit.

The car slowed to a stop in front of the quaint bed and breakfast at which we'd be spending the weekend, and Liza was at our side in an instant. With one hand on the opened door, she extended the other toward me to help me out of the vehicle. With my voluminous skirts, I really did need assistance, but even if I hadn't, I wasn't going to pass up the opportunity to make even the smallest connection with her.

Liza gripped my hand, letting her fingertips softly swipe across my palm, and I had to bite back a purr. That small stroke sent tingles down my spine. I didn't let go of her, even after I was out of the car and standing beside her on the cobblestone driveway. The building tension between us had my senses on high alert; her touch was as hypnotic as her scent, a subtle fragrance laced with notes of amber and spice.

The muted, bluish lights at the front of the inn coupled with the silvery moon to give Liza's skin an ethereal glow. But all angelic comparisons ended there. With blood-red lips and a devious gleam in her eyes, she was the embodiment of a million wicked promises. I felt my nipples, erect and sensitive, straining against my cotton chemise, and a pulsing ache had consumed my cunt. I wasn't certain what Dan and I were about to get into, but I didn't care. I was already under Liza's spell—willing to do whatever it took to fulfill her dirty desires.

As those thoughts swirled through my mind, Dan came up behind me. His breath was hot on the back of my neck, causing goose bumps to pebble my flesh. My husband slid his arms around my waist, and I saw Liza's eyes flit from my face to his. She looked as if she was carefully considering her words—and carefully considering us.

"So, shall we head inside?" she asked, her voice husky with barely concealed need. Not waiting for an answer, she turned on her heels and headed toward the inn.

I turned to Dan, who looked as bemused as he was aroused. "You game?" I asked, checking with him one last time before we forged ahead.

"Always," he answered, before dipping his head down to kiss me. The touch and taste of his familiar lips grounded me before we headed off toward the unknown.

Liza was patiently waiting for us inside, flashing a filthy smile when she saw us enter hand in hand. Dan led the way up the stairs, with Liza and me following close behind. She kept her hand on my back, and though I couldn't feel the warmth of her flesh through my many layers of clothes, I felt a gentle pressure as she guided me upward.

Liza was the last to enter our suite, shutting the door and flicking the lock with enough flair that I could hear the satisfying click of metal, so similar to the snick of locking handcuffs that my pussy instantly moistened.

Liza stalked toward me, extending a slender hand and running her fingers down my cheek, the soft scrape of her nails making my flesh tingle. My eyes fluttered closed as my face heated—a warmth that slid down my body and settled into my sex. My clit was pulsing in time with my pounding heart; I was a giant throbbing tangle of need.

"All this velvet and lace," she whispered as she circled my body. "You're like a lovely present just for me."

As Liza stood behind me—unwrapping her gift—Dan approached me from the front. With a gentle hand, he tilted my chin upward. We shared a long, deep kiss as Liza's deft fingers made quick work of my lacings, each tugging movement shifting my corset top and teasing my nipples. I moaned softly into Dan's mouth, unable to keep my pleasure to myself. In that instant, he broke our lip-lock and pulled away from me, but it was only to assist Liza in stripping me completely. Corset, chemise, crinolines and gown. Each layer fell away from my body like so many petals falling from a flower, until I was clad in nothing but my boots.

Though I'd been freed from my tightly cinched top, my breathing was still shallow, and it grew even more so when Liza embraced me. Her small breasts flattened against my back, the butter-soft leather of her corset whispering against my flesh as she writhed against me. She rhythmically rocked her body, her hands roaming my torso, petting and caressing me as she stoked my desire.

"Daniel, strip for us. Slow. We want to watch," she commanded.

Dan was a take-charge kind of guy, so this sort of situation was new to him, but he adapted just fine. As he shucked off his waistcoat, Liza cupped my breasts and trailed kisses along my neck. But I could tell that her attention was focused on him. Mine was, too. He unbuttoned his shirt, revealing his broad chest dusted with dark hair, and Liza purred with admiration. I felt like I was looking at him for the first time through Liza's eyes.

Dan toed off his shoes, and then brought his hands to his waistband to unfasten his belt. As he popped the button on his fly, Liza pinched my nipples harshly, delivering twin bursts of pain that made me whimper. She must've liked the sound because she did it again, even harder, and the volume of my reaction increased accordingly. Daniel's head snapped up at hearing my cry, and he quirked a smile as he saw Liza give my nipples another evil twist. My breasts throbbed hotly, matching the pulse in my aching cunt.

Once my husband was naked, Liza urged him forward with a come-hither crook of her finger. She reached around me to grab hold of his hair, pulling him down to her. As they kissed over my shoulder, I was pressed tightly between their bodies, feeling the electricity sparking between them.

"Get on the bed, baby," she murmured to Dan before giving me a sideways glance. "Bridget looks like one hell of a cocksucker with those fine lips of hers—and I want to see her in action."

Heeding her words, Dan spread himself out on the mattress.

Liza, meanwhile, gave me a sharp slap on the ass, the burn only serving to fan the flames of my lust.

"Upsy-daisy, sweetheart. You're a pretty lady, but I bet you'll look even better with a dick in your mouth. Start sucking that cock."

It was hard not to laugh, but I managed. After all, I had a handsome man with a hard cock that needed sucking and a sexy blonde barking orders at me—neither of which was a laughing matter.

I settled myself on my knees between Dan's spread thighs, leaning forward to bring my lips to his. My eyes drifted shut as Dan wrapped his arms around me and we shared a tender kiss; our lips were still locked as Liza's hand delivered another harsh blow to my exposed cheeks. My immediate reaction was to rear up, but I couldn't, being held tight by Dan's embrace.

Liza grabbed the back of my hair and turned my head, so she could look directly into my eyes.

"You clearly can't follow orders and need to be taught a lesson. You weren't told to kiss him. You were told to suck his cock."

I began to move, but a firm hand on my back pushed me down against my husband. My breasts were squashed beneath me, the scratchy hair on Dan's chest enflaming my already sensitive nipples, and his erect cock pulsed against my stomach.

Dan had also begun to move, his arms sliding away to release me.

"No, you don't," she said to him. "You hold her still while she gets what she deserves."

Dan's hands returned to their place on my back as I became acutely aware of my naked and vulnerable ass. Dan's heart was pounding as wildly as mine; I could feel it thumping against my chest.

I heard the slippery rasp of fabric and waited a few minutes before I dared to turn my head in her direction. When I did, I saw that Liza had stripped out of her clothing and was now naked—except for her hat. Her small breasts were topped with puffy pink nipples, and her alabaster skin was smooth and flawless. While her beauty was stunning, what left me truly breathless was the sight of Dan's black leather belt in her hand.

Liza snapped the belt—hot, hard and sharp—across both cheeks of my ass. My lips parted in a wordless gasp of surrender. Dan gripped me more tightly, kissing the top of my head as Liza delivered another blow, which was quickly followed by more. The leather landed in measured, even strokes, taking me on a roller-coaster ride of sensations. When the belt connected with my flesh, pain shocked my senses, but it quickly faded into a deep burn that spread from my well-whipped ass to my aroused cunt. Every slap of leather made my slit just a little bit wetter, and before long, my thighs felt slippery with the undeniable evidence of my arousal. Keeping time with her strokes, I rocked my body against Dan's, increasing the pressure on his cock with every one of my movements. In the haze of my arousal, I felt his fingers skittering along my spine as he struggled to maintain his control—even as he pumped his hips upward to eke out bits of indecent pleasure.

My body felt boneless, all of the tension leaving me as I brought my full weight to bear on Dan and submitted to her fully, taking all she had to give. Sensing my complete surrender, Liza tossed the belt on the mattress, and a second later, I felt her hand caress my behind, her touch—though gentle—making me whimper.

Liza's fingers slid across my burning cheeks and down between my thighs, skidding across my lips. She pressed in deeper, gliding along my flesh and easily penetrating me.

Fucking me fast and hard, she rubbed her thumb against my clit in perfect circles. Still being held by Dan, I thrust my hips back in little bursts of movement, wanting it deeper, harder. At the same time, Dan's hands were clutching my back tightly and his breathing was becoming as erratic as mine. My belly felt slick from the precome that was leaking from his cock, making our bodies slide and writhe with even greater ease.

When I was on the verge of coming, Liza stilled her hand. I turned to her, ready to beg—ready to say anything that would give me the pleasure that I craved.

"Are you ready to suck that cock now?"

"Yes, Ma'am," I answered, my voice sounding as shaky as my body felt.

With a nod of her head, she instructed Dan to release me and with some effort, I slid downward to take his dick in my mouth. Wild with unfettered lust, I pumped my lips up and down his shaft. Dan was so worked up that he had to slow me down to keep from climaxing too soon. I eased my pace, stopping my mouth's movement when he seemed close to coming again and simply holding him between my lips as I swirled my tongue around his cockhead.

At the same time, Liza gripped his cock at the base, stroking it gently.

She kissed my cheek and whispered, "Time to take a ride, baby."

I pulled back, the taste of Dan's dick still on my tongue, as Liza held his shaft steady for me. I lowered myself onto his erection, my cunt already primed from all of her hard work. She pulled her hand away, and I seated myself firmly on my husband's erection. As I enjoyed the sensation of Dan's cock filling me for the first time that night, Liza joined us on the bed by straddling his head.

Liza was facing me, and as Dan grabbed her slender hips and pulled her pussy to his lips, I saw her eyes flutter closed. I began to ride Dan's cock, inspired by the ecstasy that was etched on her face, as he lapped at her slit. The black cap still sat atop Liza's head, but it was now slightly askew. She danced lewdly on Dan's face, taking as much pleasure as she could get from his lips and tongue. Matching her rhythm, I ground my pussy against Dan's body, until a climax fluttered through me, stealing my breath. He must've felt my cunt pulsing around his shaft because he groaned loudly, his cries no doubt vibrating against Liza's wet sex. It was the dirtiest chain reaction I'd ever witnessed, with my orgasm setting off Dan's, which made Liza's follow soon thereafter. She was gorgeous when she finally came, her pale skin flushed as she gave in to her lust and shared in our pleasure.

I have to admit that I hadn't thought our wedding night would include a kinky threeway, but I was thrilled by how the evening had turned out. I'm glad we let Liza steer us down the road less traveled.

WARM FRONT

Heidi Champa

This storm is a big fucking deal."

The room was silent as Don continued, his serious tone soon devolving into his usual sardonic delivery.

"Anyone who doesn't want to be stuck here all night, better go now. The snow's getting worse. If you're not essential to tonight's broadcast, get out now while you still can. And, for god's sake, be safe out there. It's too expensive to replace any of you."

A small laugh went through the room and suddenly the gravity of the situation hit us all.

"We'll keep everyone posted about tomorrow. Until then, scram!"

A chorus of groans from those left behind was overshadowed by the giddy conversations of those that were getting to leave work early for the day. With his words, Don, our station manager, managed to make and ruin nights all at the same time.

"Those of you lucky enough to be essential, I hope you're ready to stay here all night. Remember, the couch in the lobby only fits two people. The rest of you will have to make do in the conference room chairs."

The snow had been steadily falling all day and the roads were getting closer to impassible every minute. Everyone else who was, like me, essential to making news shows run, looked defeated and angry. I was quite the opposite. I'd been waiting for a snow day like this for weeks. Winter had been stingy thus far, giving us only a few inches here and there for the last month. But I was finally getting the blizzard I wanted and needed. My scheming mind was distracted by a grumpy voice.

"What the hell are you smiling about, Kenna?"

I hadn't realized that I was grinning like a fool until my coworker David brought it to my attention. He seemed less than thrilled at our predicament, but as head of graphics, he had no choice but to stay. Even though I was a lowly teleprompter operator, without me, the anchors would have nothing to say. David's scowl deepened and I wiped the smile from my face before I spoke.

"I just like snow. It'll be fun. You'll see."

"Right. Just my idea of a good time. Curled up in a horrible chair all night, freezing our butts off because the station is too cheap to turn the heat up past sixty-five at night. Yeah, gonna be a real hoot."

He looked at me with disbelief and shook his head as he turned back to his computer screen. At that moment, Jacob Weisman, resident meteorologist and the hottie who had haunted my fantasy life for nearly two years walked into the room, his microphone in one hand, a few pieces of paper in the other. Our eyes met and he shot me the million-dollar smile the people of our town had come to rely on for all their weather needs. He winked right before he pushed open the door to the frosty air outside and left me breathless.

When he returned a few minutes later, I nearly gasped when I saw him. He looked so damn good covered in tiny flecks of white, his deep, dark hair dotted with winter wonderland. After a quick glance my way, he was gone again, and I was left trying in vain to stay focused on the task in front of me.

I knew the rest of the night would tick by slowly, but it was becoming interminable. The delicious anticipation of putting my long-held plan into action was tempered by the mundane tasks of my job and the mindless chatter that was going on all around me. The evening newscast went by without much fanfare, everyone already looking ahead to the eleven o'clock broadcast. In the short break we had in between the chaos, I took a moment to stare out the window, watching everything turn into a sea of white calm. The roads were deserted and the only noise was the soft hum of the ancient furnace pumping out a dry, warm breeze.

"Beautiful, isn't it, Kenna?"

I'd jumped at Jacob's voice, but as he got closer to me, my heart kept pounding for a completely different reason. He stood a couple of inches too close and focused his eyes straight ahead.

"Yeah, it's amazing. Probably not much fun to stand in doing a weather report though, huh?"

"You'd be surprised. I love it. Especially on nights like tonight. I do love this job. Except for the whole sleeping in my office thing. Not great."

"At least you have an office. The rest of us end up on a pile of giveaway windbreakers in the conference room."

His laughter was quiet, but it still managed to make my insides turn over.

"Well, maybe we should see if we have any of those extra fleece blankets from the last promotion. They were pretty warm. They might work a little better than those awful windbreakers."

Anyone else's sarcasm would have irritated me at that moment, but with Jacob, it only made him more endearing. In that moment, I decided to be bold. I turned to face him, ready to say or do something stupid, but before I could, we were interrupted.

"Jake, we need you for a minute."

It was some production assistant whose name I could never quite remember. If looks could kill, he'd have been on the floor in a pool of blood, but instead Jacob smiled at me before laying a hand on my shoulder. It was innocent enough, but felt anything but.

"Well, see you later, Kenna. I'll get my report for the prompter to you in about an hour. I'm not sure if you've heard, but it's snowing like crazy tonight."

"Thanks for the heads-up."

"Hey, I'm not the best weatherman in the biz for nothing."

He disappeared down the corridor, leaving me shivering by the window. And I wasn't even cold.

The show went by without a hitch, most of the half hour dedicated to the snowstorm. Jacob was in all his glory, getting to go on and on about radar, accumulation and blizzard-like conditions. I watched his every move from the control room, slowly turning the knob that fed the information to the little screen below the camera that he read with such ease.

When the broadcast came to an end, there was the usual bullshit session for all the anchors after, which on nights like this included a few drinks to pass the time until everyone retreated to his or her office to try and get some sleep. Jacob would have to be up bright and early for the morning broadcast, filling in for the morning meteorologist who was already snowed in at his farm out of town.

I sat on the cool leather couch in Jacob's office waiting in the dark with one of the station's fleece blankets around my shoulders. He was right; they were warm. I could hear voices in the distance and I felt every hair on the back of my neck stand up. As the footsteps in the hall got closer, I could hardly believe that my plan was finally coming to fruition.

The door pushed open and before he had the chance to flick on the lights, I spoke up.

"Hi."

It was his turn to jump from surprise, but he recovered quickly. Except for the hand that involuntarily flew to his chest.

"Kenna? I wasn't expecting to see you here."

I moved a bit on the couch, trying to keep myself calm. My whole body was flushed with heat and my throat was suddenly dry.

"I couldn't face a night in the conference room."

I expected him to protest or throw me out without another word, but instead he plunked down next to me on the couch, rubbing his hands up and down the thighs of his expensive suit pants.

"I don't blame you. Although I see you managed to find a blanket. Where was it hiding?"

"The storage closet next to the old tape room."

"Good to know. Did you bring me one?"

"Nope."

The corner of Jacob's mouth twitched right before he smiled. I could smell his cologne and every inch of my body was tingling. My heart nearly stopped when he slid across the leather until he was right next to me.

"Was the plan to share, then?"

It was my chance. All I had to do was open my mouth and say yes. He was being deliberately provocative and goddamn was it making my pussy wet. I gathered every ounce of my strength and licked my lips, trying to keep my voice from shaking.

"I thought it might make sense, you know, since we'll be sharing the couch, too."

His eyebrows raised and I waited for the rejection I knew was coming. Instead, he grabbed my arm and pulled me into his lap, my legs on either side of his before I knew what was happening. Jacob ran his large hands up my back and down again, squeezing my ass as he drew me closer.

"If we're going to share, then maybe we should get a bit more comfortable."

Before I could answer him, he pulled me closer still, his soft lips gently teasing mine before kissing me hard. I gripped his shoulders as I felt his tongue sweep into my mouth. His hands moved to the hem of my blouse and starting lifting it. Our lips parted long enough to let my shirt pass over my head and land somewhere on the floor behind me. Jacob's eyes dropped to my lace bra, and I felt a fresh wash of moisture between my legs.

I was frozen as he reached up with two fingers and flipped open the front clasp, exposing me. The chill in the air made my nipples peak, which Jacob assisted with the tips of his fingers. When his lips closed around one sensitive nub, I couldn't stop myself from running my fingers through his TV-perfect hair. He slumped back into the couch and started unbuttoning his shirt, his eyes fixed on mine.

"So, if there hadn't been a blizzard tonight, would we be here right now?"

I eased off his lap until my knees hit the floor. Growing impatient with his slow undressing, I pushed his hands aside and finished opening his shirt in record time.

"Does it really matter, Jacob?"

"No. But remind me to thank Don for making you such an essential part of our newscast."

I threw his shirt over my shoulder and practically ripped the white T-shirt from his muscled torso. My eyes dropped to the flash of silver in his belt buckle and in my moment's hesitation, Jacob opened his pants, exposing the proud curve of his erection pressing against the black fabric of his boxer-briefs. His pricey wool pants were soon alongside the rest of his clothes on the ugly station carpet. All that stood between me and his cock was a flimsy bit of cotton. I'd lost count of the minutes and hours I'd wasted at work imagining this very thing. As I peeled the last layer of impediment away, my breath caught in my throat at the sight of his gorgeous dick, hard and thick.

Wrapping my hand around the base, I took the tip into my mouth, closing my eyes as he let out a deep sigh and slouched down on the leather. I laved my tongue over every inch of him, taking the time to suck each of his balls into my mouth, before enveloping him completely down my throat.

"Fuck. That feels so good."

His hand twined in my hair, the gentle tug making my hand drop into my panties. I was soaking wet and as my fingers slid over my swollen clit, I moaned around his cock. Just as my tongue swirled around the flared tip of his cock, he shifted away from me. Looking up at him, I saw a quirky grin on his face.

"Your turn, Kenna."

He pulled me to my feet and playfully shoved me back on the couch, right on top of my stolen fleece blanket. My pants and thong were gone in an instant and Jacob spread my legs wide, taking his time running his hands up the insides of my thighs. I stared at the water-stained ceiling as he parted my pussy lips with his thumbs, my whole body trembling in anticipation and lust. The tip of a finger slid inside me at the same time his lips made contact with my clit, making my back arch off the couch. He teased and toyed with me, pouring pure gasoline onto an already raging fire. As he probed me deeper, his husky voice rang out in the small space.

"God, you taste so good. Even better than I imagined."

I gasped as he took the words from my brain, the soft swirl of his tongue making it impossible to even contemplate a response. My hips moved without my consent, pushing me ever closer to the edge. Jacob's rhythm was ever changing and when I felt one finger become two inside me, I couldn't stop the moans from coming out of my mouth. My logical brain knew I should be quiet, but it seemed beyond me at that moment. Just as the pleasure started to overwhelm me, Jacob disappeared from between my legs. I propped myself up on my elbows just in time to see him returning from his desk with a condom in his hand.

"Sorry for the delay. I wasn't exactly expecting this tonight."

"Says the guy with condoms in his desk at work."

"Call it wishful thinking. I've always wanted to fuck in here."

"Glad I could help."

"Me too."

He kissed me and sat down on the sofa and I watched as he rolled the condom onto his cock. Once again, he pulled me into his lap, my wet cunt mere inches away from the head of his dick. Our lips met again as he tried to urge me on, but I was enjoying his torment a bit too much to give in so soon. He sighed as I nibbled his neck, letting the space between us diminish until I felt him between my swollen lips. I tilted my hips and let him rub over my clit before smiling down at him.

"Please, Kenna. You're killing me. Haven't I waited long enough for you?"

I eased down onto his cock, his mouth falling open as I finished my slow slide.

"I think we've both waited long enough."

I expected a frenzied fuck, but instead we moved slowly, deliberately, as if to relish each sensation. Jacob's hands cupped my tits, his thumbs strafing my nipples as he moved in and out of me. The friction of my clit rubbing against him was exquisite, as were his lips around my nipple, sucking and licking.

"Jacob."

His name came out of my mouth in a whisper, but he replied with a groan. We started to move faster, our bodies both careening toward the edge with abandon. I cast a glance toward the window, where the snow was still falling softly just beyond the glass. He took my attention back with a hard kiss, his hands cupping my ass as he fucked me. I swiveled my hips hard against him, giving me just the nudge I needed. My head fell back, and my moans grew choked and broken as I came. Jacob held me through each shudder, until I couldn't move anymore, my body heavy and spent. He thrust into me one last time, grunting softly against the crook of my neck, his embrace tightening as he came.

It took all the rest of my strength to climb off him and collapse onto the couch. After Jacob cleaned up, he lay down beside me, pulling the fleece blanket over us both. Our bodies entwined as my eyes fell closed; his fingers stroked up and down my back.

"Jesus, Kenna. That was amazing."

"Right back at you, Jacob. Sorry I kept you up so late."

"It's okay. Jan in makeup will just have to work extra hard tomorrow."

He kissed me softly and pulled me tighter.

"It's a shame this snow's going to stop by morning."

"Why's that?"

"Because it would have been nice to be snowed in with you again tomorrow night."

"Well, maybe we'll get another storm soon."

He chuckled, and I could feel the vibrations through his chest.

"It's funny you should say that. There's supposed to be another storm front coming through this weekend. Maybe just to be safe, you should come to my place after work on Friday. You know, just in case we get trapped again."

"Sounds like a plan."

"And, Kenna?"

"Yeah?"

"Don't forget to bring a blanket."

DOCTOR'S ORDERS

Sasha White

It was the car that first caught my attention. A red 1974 Triumph convertible. Even though it was my first day of work at the hospital, and I was late, my feet slowed as I walked past that car. I've always loved a fast ride, and that car promised one.

It didn't take long to learn who it belonged to either. Dr. Tyler was the name all the nurses whispered with a giggle and a sigh. He was handsome, charming and a neurologist. He wasn't a hot young stud like television's McDreamy; he was better. And as the months passed, I learned more. Dr. Ty played golf and the piano with equal ease. He spoke to the staff with kindness, not condescension. And when he serenaded his date with his smooth deep voice at the hospital's Christmas party, there wasn't a dry pair of panties in the room by the time he was done. Even the older nurses watched him with a gleam of desire in their eyes.

Me? I stayed away from him as best I could. Strong, intelligent men were a weakness of mine, but I'd learned early on in my career not to play where I work.

That didn't stop me from fantasizing though, and after the shit week I'd just been through, a Dr. Ty fix was just what I needed.

I heard his laugh as soon as I entered the lecture theater, and my pussy gave a little quiver of anticipation. After settling into a seat in the back corner, I sent a quick prayer skyward that no one would sit nearby, and watched the small group of men near the stage. They all wore the white coats of their shared profession, the same one almost everyone else in the theater wore. The joy of working in a teaching hospital was being able to attend lectures on specialties that weren't my own.

At this point in time I really didn't care what the topic was, all I cared about was sitting in the back staring at Dr. Ty and listening to that smooth voice use big fifty-dollar words as I did my best not to come in my pants. At the end of his lecture I stayed in my seat, head back and eyes closed as everyone around me streamed out of the room. When I was surrounded by silence, I opened my eyes and straightened up in preparation for leaving, only to find the man himself standing in front of me.

"I'm sorry to be so boring as to put you to sleep, Dr. Barrow," he said.

Heat crept up my neck and I debated what to do next. I knew what I should do, and it wasn't what I wanted to do. "I wasn't sleeping, Doctor," I replied, hoping he'd take the bait.

"What were you doing?"

I stood, a small smile playing at my lips. "Fantasizing," I said, then walked away.

Come on, come on, come on, I thought as I neared the theater's exit. *Don't let me down Dr. Ty.*

"Dr. Barrow," he called out, sending a surge of pleasure through my veins. "May I ask what you were fantasizing about?"

I turned at the exit and faced him. He was less than ten feet away, his head tilted slightly, his lips curled in an inviting smile. It wasn't just his voice that turned me on, or the big words. It was the glasses, the intelligence that gleamed in his eyes and the brain that made him such a success in his field. When I said he wasn't McDreamy, I meant it. He wasn't some thirtysomething stud with a full head of thick, curly hair to wrap my fingers in and a rock-hard body to ride all night long. He was a good fifteen years older than me, his hair was a little graying and his waistline a little soft. But he was smart, and strong, and as I watched him walk toward me with that flirty little grin, all I could think about was getting him on my gynecological table, strapping his feet into the stirrups and turning that powerful brain to mush.

"I'm not much of a talker, Doctor, but if you feel you're up to it, I'd be happy to show you."

His eyebrows jumped and his eyes brightened at my challenge. My heart pounded and my insides quivered as I waited for his answer. I was breaking one of my own rules, but at this point I just didn't give a fuck.

"What exactly would showing me entail?" he asked as he sauntered forward.

"Getting naked," I replied. "Beyond that you'll just have to follow me to find out."

That said, I left the theater. Chest tight and thighs slick with desire, I strode down the hallway toward the exam room I'd just been dreaming of. Solid footsteps followed me, and I breathed a sigh of relief. He was coming. This was going to happen.

He surprised me by not flinching when he followed me into the examining room and saw me standing next to the gynecological table, a hand caressing one of the stirrups. "Ready?" I asked.

He moved forward as if to kiss me, and I stepped back, a hand on his chest. "Oh, no. This isn't about romance, Doctor. It's about pleasure."

"Excuse me?"

"Strip."

Since I was already shrugging out of my lab coat and reaching for the buttons on my blouse, he quickly followed suit. When he was naked, he moved toward me, hands reaching. Again, I stepped away.

"Linda?" he asked.

"My fantasy, right, Dr. Ty?"

"Yes," he said, sounding just the tiniest bit unsure.

I gestured to the exam table. This was a make it or break it moment. "Hop up and put your feet in the stirrups then, please."

We stared at each other for a moment, and the gentle throb between my legs kicked up a notch. Just when I thought he was going to reach for his pants and leave, Ty took a deep breath and climbed up onto the table.

My breath caught in my throat and I grinned at him. "You've always been sexy, Tyler, but never have I wanted you more than I do right now," I said.

His hard-on had deflated, but my words made his cock twitch again, and I started slow. Gliding my hands up his naked legs, I was sure to keep my touch light so that the hair dusting his skin stood up to tickle the palm of my hand. I ignored the softness of his cock and continued up over his chest to toy with his nipples. His hands twitched on the table, and I knew he was unsure of what to do with them. Curious to see what he would do, I didn't offer any direction. I tickled the shell of his ear and walked around the table to the other side. Only when I reached the end of the table again and stood between his spread thighs did he speak, his voice quivering just a little.

"What are you planning on doing down there, Dr. Barrow?"

The anxious question sent a shiver of delight through me. Bending forward I nuzzled my cheek against his inner thigh, and let my breath tease the sensitive skin of his balls as I answered.

"I plan on making you speechless with pleasure, Dr. Tyler," I replied before taking his cock in my mouth and sucking.

There's something beyond erotic about taking a man in your mouth when he's soft and feeling him grow inside you. I could count his heartbeats by the throb of his cock as it stiffened against my tongue. I wrapped my lips around him and took him as deep as I could. Soon, his hardness filled my mouth and my hand was gripping the base, holding Ty still as he tried to thrust.

Now that he was hard, it was time to play.

Stepping back, I went for my purse. It didn't take long to find what I was looking for, and the sound of the Velcro tearing open echoed loudly in the room. I dug the fingertip vibrator out of the little pack and slipped it on. Holding up my hand to show Ty what it was, I walked back to where he lay.

"What's that?" he asked, ignoring the condom packet I tossed on his belly.

"It's a vibrator," I replied. "Most stores advertise it as a massager for headaches and neck pain, which it does work on, but because of its size the options for use are only as endless as your imagination."

I pressed the tiny switch and watched Ty's face for a reaction as I slowly lowered my covered fingertip toward his hard nipple. He gasped when I brushed it lightly over the rigid tip. Encouraged, I brushed it once again, more firmly. No gasp this time, but his mouth opened soundlessly and his body arched against my hand, wanting firmer pressure.

Teasing him, I brushed my covered fingertip over his other

nipple and placed my lips on the abandoned one, sucking gently at first, and then strongly, before starting to nibble sharply with my teeth at the same time as I rolled the other nipple between the vibrating pad and my thumb. The silence continued to be broken only by the occasional gasp or moan of pleasure.

I felt his hand for the first time then. His body lay still as he let me play, but one of his hands slid up the back of my thigh and over my ass, where his fingers dug into the plump cheeks before relaxing again. I continued to lick and nibble at his chest, my hand traveling south as his fingers gripped, then relaxed, like a cat kneading a pillow before it lies down.

The muscles in his thighs tensed when I cupped his balls, and a shiver ran through him. He lifted his hips with a groan and twisted his body, lifting me up onto the table to straddle his face. Firm hands gripped my hips and he pulled me down until I was almost sitting on his face. His tongue thrust between my swollen pussy lips and licked up and down, learning the dips and swells between the slick folds until he nudged against my entrance. I shifted my weight until I was lying between his thighs, and he could feel my breath on his eager cock.

My tongue snaked out and swiped a taste of the precome leaking from the tiny opening. "Oh yeah," he groaned.

Using the forefinger and thumb of my free hand I circled the base of his cock and pulled it away from his belly before placing a long, slow, wet lick up the underside to the head. I licked it like a lollipop for a few seconds before finally taking him completely into my mouth and going to work. I began slowly, with firm strokes up and down and gentle suction, my tongue playing along his shaft inside my mouth, but his own busy tongue kept distracting me. I knew I should be going slower, should be enjoying having this man naked in front of me, toying with him, teasing him and stoking his passion higher and higher until he begged. But right then, I was the one who was ready to beg.

Determined to give as good as I got, I reached around his leg and pressed my vibrating fingertip against the soft skin between his balls and his asshole as I humped his face.

"Ooh god," he moaned. "You're good."

His cock was pulsing against my tongue, and I knew he couldn't take much more. I pressed my fingertip firmly against the tender area under his balls before sliding it toward his puckered hole and picking up the speed of my strokes. His cock throbbed against my tongue and his balls pulled up against my chin, signaling he was about to come. I tightened my grip on the base of his cock and pulled back. "Not yet, stud," I warned.

A soft "Arrgghhhh," was the frustrated response I got.

Sitting up, I reached for the condom pack, ripped it open and rolled it down his impressive length. Shuffling forward on my knees, I gripped his cock in one hand and braced my body with the other on one of his knees before impaling myself on his shaft.

"Ugh!" he grunted.

"God, you feel good!" I sighed.

"Oh yeah, baby. That's it. Ride me." Ty's hands snaked down and gripped my hips to hold me as he used his feet in the stirrups to brace himself and thrust upward. I moaned with each thrust as he hit deep inside me, and I slid my hand between us. A shock of pleasure ripped through me when the vibrator pulsed against my clit, and my pussy clenched.

"What?" Ty grunted.

His hands gripped my waist and his hips pistoned up and down as he panted like a freight train. His thick cock rammed up into me again and again and my cunt tightened, the first tremors of an orgasm gaining power. I was quickly losing my sanity as pleasure washed over me, so I reached between his spread thighs and played my fingertip over his tightly puckered hole.

"Oh shit," Ty cried. "Oh fuck."

Triumph filled me as I realized I'd done what I'd been fantasizing about for months. I'd reduced the charming and intelligent Dr. Tyler to animalistic grunts and monosyllabic groans of pleasure.

His hips pumped harder and my finger slid past the tight ring of his rear entrance. "Come on, Ty, let go," I urged. "Feel me. Fuck me hard."

He grunted, once, twice, pulling me down hard as he thrust so deep pleasure and pain blurred and I came.

"Oh yeah," he gasped. "Oh yeah, oh yeah."

"Ohhh," I cried out, shuddering and melting on top of him.

There was silence for a few moments, then I heard that smooth, deep voice of his. "I'm sorry," he said.

That puzzled me. I struggled to come back to myself, to think, to make sense of his words. "Why?" I mumbled. "Why are you sorry?"

"I'm sorry my lecture was so boring as to put you to sleep, Dr. Barrow."

My spine snapped straight and my eyes flew open to see Dr. Tyler standing directly in front of me, fully clothed, still in the now-empty theater.

Heat crept up my neck, and I debated what to do next. I knew what I should do, and it wasn't what I wanted to do. "I wasn't sleeping, Doctor," I replied, hoping he'd take the bait.

"What were you doing?"

I stood, a small smile playing at my lips. "Fantasizing," I said, then walked away.

Come on, come on, come on, I thought as I neared the theater's exit. *Don't let me down, Dr. Ty.*

JUST A LITTLE TENDERNESS

A. M. Hartnett

The part of my job that I hated the most was covering the reception desk. I'd plunk my ass at the front desk for an hour and avoid making eye contact with the couriers and walk-ins. The pest-control guy made small talk with my breasts. The guy who delivered office products grunted at me. Occasionally we'd have an actual client walk in, but that was rare.

After an hour I'd return to my desk, bitchier than ever over the time I had lost doing something as irritating as reception. I had paper to push, numbers to crunch and about seventy blogs to read when I was sure no one was looking.

Fridays were different. Friday was the day Eric delivered the water.

Ah, Eric.

He was a brown-haired, blue-eyed, bearded dream. He'd come charging through the front door with one or two big jugs propped on his shoulders. His muscles strained and sweat popped out on his brow as he zoomed past me toward the kitchen. When he came back, he'd make flirty small talk with me and I'd be lit up for the rest of the afternoon.

From the boyfriend who had dumped me for a neighbor he had once cruelly referred to as the Bearded Lady, to the online date who had waited until after we had sex to tell me he wasn't feeling it, to the bus driver I had seen for eight months who seemed to appreciate teenaged girls a little too much, some real winners had come and gone while Eric had been the only male constant in my life since I'd started working at C&E.

He was reliable. He knew I had named my car Shirley. He knew I liked books about Vikings. He always looked me in the eyes when he talked to me, even when I was wearing a V-neck.

Eric, who made my insides squishy.

Eric, who on that Friday hobbled into the office with a cast on his leg and a crutch under his armpit. He had one bottle of water precariously perched on his shoulder.

"Eric, what the hell?" I shot around the desk, but he held up his free hand.

"I'm good. I've been doing this all day." He let the bottle slide to the floor and propped his crutch against the desk. Huffing, he lifted his shirt and wiped his face.

I was momentarily disarmed by the sight of his brawny upper body, but curiosity trumped horniness. "What happened?"

"Soccer. There was flipping involved, and a little bit of flying."

"Why are you even working?"

"They couldn't get anyone to cover my shift," he said, then grinned. "Besides, you'd go thirsty if I didn't show up."

"You're the one who looks like he could use a drink. Come sit down for five minutes."

I quickly transferred the phone to the break room and helped him along. I figured I could keep an eye on the door, but I doubted anyone would come in. In addition to being the highlight of the week, Eric was also usually the last service guy to come into the office for the day.

"Here. Sit. *Sit.*" I made him put his ass in the task chair that sat in front of the staff computer. He winced as he went down. "Please tell me you don't work the weekend too."

"Fuck no; we have a crew for that." His hand flew up to his mouth. "Sorry."

"Don't be. The office is empty. Besides, no one ever comes back early on Fridays."

The water cooler gurgled as I filled a glass. Upon handing it over to him, I looked down at his cast. "That's pathetic. It's not signed."

Once he drank down every drop, he passed the glass back to me. "I'm not ten years old, and it's too hot to wear pants over them."

"I'm going to sign it right after I bring the water in here."

"Dayna, don't. That's my job."

"Quiet, you." I ignored him and returned to reception. Moments later, I was back, rolling the water in front of me and biting down on a purple sharpie.

"Just don't draw flowers or hearts or anything on it."

I rolled my eyes as I went on my knees in front of him. "I'm just going to write *get well* and maybe draw a penis."

Eric laughed, a sound that just wonderfully rumbled on and on. "You know, I've never said anything because you might think I was an asshole, but I've always wanted to see if you would hang out one night."

I uncapped the marker. "Why would I think you were an asshole?"

"I'm a water guy. Why would you want to hang out with me?"

"Jesus, what do you think I do here? Crumpets and tea while I boss around my peons? You probably make more than I do." I rocked back on my knees. "Where do you want it?"

The suggestion in my words wasn't intentional, but just the same heat rushed into my cheeks while his smile turned curious.

"Middle of the thigh," he said quietly. "You've got lots of room to write."

I poised the marker over the hard plaster and for a few seconds chewed my lip. "I just drew a blank."

"It must be my animal magnetism paralyzing you. That or the proximity to my cock."

I frowned. "That is inappropriate and shocking office language, though now that you mention it, this is a little porny, isn't it?"

"I guess so. The secretary and the delivery boy, empty office, you on your knees like that..."

Tingles started at the base of my neck and danced over my shoulders. "With you helpless and in need of some TLC."

His proximity had only been somewhat distracting up until this moment, but now it was heavy and all around me. That creeping arousal moved through my body. My breath came in short bursts. My nipples tightened against my bra.

"What kind of TLC did you have in mind?" he asked.

My cheeks pricked with spots of heat. "I think we both know what I have in mind."

The marker dropped to the floor as Eric reached forward. He wriggled the top button of my blouse free, and if I hadn't already been on my knees, by the time he'd opened up my shirt to the belly button, I would have dropped to the floor.

Eric slipped his hands inside the gap and fingered the black lace edges of my pink bra. "I figured you wore something like this under your clothes. Always a great fantasy to jerk off to."

I slid my hands over his thighs, over hairy flesh on one side and cold plaster on the other until I reached the hem of his shorts. "You want to know what I jerk off to?"

"You bet I do."

"The thought of you jerking off."

The thin bra straps slipped and the cups buckled just enough for him to get his hands inside. Rough fingers tugged my nipples and the sting drew a throaty curse from deep inside me.

I felt a little desperate as I continued up his thighs to the bulge that threatened to split his zipper. "I'd picture you standing at the foot of my bed, stroking your hard-on while you watched me do the same to myself."

The rough play with my nipples had amped up all the hot energy running through me. I wanted his cock loose and in my hands and I wanted it now. I could hardly focus as I worked his fly.

Another pinch. "Do you wear anything while you do that?"

"I'm a masturbatory drama queen." I split open his fly and reached up under his shirt. "I wear the same thing I wear if I'm going to be fucked: bra and panties, garters and stockings."

Eric lifted his ass. I yanked his shorts and boxers to where the cast met his thighs. A good six inches of utterly mouthwatering flesh sprang up.

"That's how I pictured you," he said, and leaned back in the chair, "only when I'm thinking about it, I'm rubbing you through your panties instead of watching."

"This is *definitely* inappropriate workplace language," I teased as I took hold of his dick, "but since no one is around to hear it..."

I swirled my tongue around the smooth head, licking the whole circumference and then repeating the action in the opposite direction. It didn't even occur to me to shush Eric as he hung his head back and moaned. After all, Friday was dead day. I figured we would have the office to ourselves for an hour.

Eyes closed, I sucked him like he was one of those fat Christmas candy canes. He was mine to play with, yet I didn't want to tease him too much. I wanted him ready. I knew that as soon as I had him balls deep I'd be ready to explode.

"Phone," he said in a grunt. I didn't stop. The call could damn well go to the service.

His cock throbbed as I worked him deeper. In spite of the cast on one leg, he put all his effort into using the other to rise up out of the seat and meet the pace with which I bobbed my head.

Sliding him out of my mouth with a wet pop, I drew back and grinned up at him. "I'm convinced that whoever made these shitty chairs left the arms off because he knew they would get in the way during office quickies."

"That sounds so promising." He made a grab for me as I went around the chair, but sank helplessly back as I started to push.

Zoom, down the hall to my office we went. If anyone came in we'd be concealed, and I could explain my absence by saying I had to take a confidential call from an irate client; we had enough hotheads that no one would question it.

With the door closed and locked behind us, I lifted the phone from the receiver and selected a line as cover, then turned to Eric with a grin.

"Ready to see what else I have on under here, perv?" I did a little wiggle as I unclasped my skirt.

He placed his hands behind his head so his elbows stuck out like wings and he grinned. "I suppose a little striptease won't hurt."

The shirt crumpled at my feet. My skirt ended up over the file cabinet. I half-turned to show off my white and black thong, and Eric dropped one of his hands to his lap and his cock all but disappeared into his fist.

"It's killing me that I can't get up and undress you myself."

His gaze followed me like a caress as I rolled my chair from the desk to face his. I slid down to mirror his pose, my back flat against the seat and my legs outstretched, and ran my hands slowly along my inner thighs. The closer I got, the more I could feel the damp heat coming from my pussy.

"I feel like I need to be gentle with you," I said, my fingers brushing my wet crotch, "but I don't want to get you too excited while I give you a show. Pace yourself."

Eric wet his lips. "It would probably be best if it's less of a show and more of a preview."

Hotter than ever under his stare, I rubbed my finger around and around where my clit pressed against my panties.

A strange and wonderful feeling simmered beneath my skin. As much as I had imagined doing it for Eric and a dozen men before him, I'd never touched myself in front of someone else for this purpose. To get off while going down, yes, but never to show off.

Even as I heard the sounds of my coworkers returning, I wasn't fazed. It was all about the delightful rings throbbing outward from my clit.

The second I slipped my fingers underneath my panties and went to the knuckle, Eric jerked upright in the chair. "In my left pocket, there's a condom in the metal tin."

Abandoning my solo play, I scrambled with the condom concealed in an Altoids tin, ripped into the wrapping, and snapped it on his dick. My panties landed on the mouse pad, bringing my computer to boring spreadsheet-filled life.

I straddled him, my fingers digging into his shoulders to steady myself until the fat tip plugged me.

"No moaning, no nothing," I said in a hissed whisper.

I nearly broke the rule I had made when he grasped my hips and pulled me down.

"Sweet fucking Jesus." Eric wriggled underneath me, but his cast prevented him from moving much at all. I had all of the momentum.

With my heels digging into the cheap carpet, I rode him hard and fast. I buried my face in his damp neck, moaning just low enough that he could hear it. The rustle of his clothes and the wet sound of my body taking his in seemed so loud. My lungs burned to keep from screaming as I fucked us both into white-hot oblivion.

The friction of that thick cock between my slippery walls was sweet enough, but the way I was seated meant every thrust down gave me the added friction of his pubic hair against my clit. I ground down on him faster and faster, my cunt so hot and throbbing I felt like a firecracker.

"Coming," I groaned against his skin. I wrapped my arms around his shoulders and closed my eyes as my pussy throbbed around his dick. My body echoed my words, igniting sparks that sizzled through my whole body.

Eric's grip on my ass tightened. He lifted me up and down, up and down. Struggling through the haze of my lingering orgasm, I held on to him and kept up the momentum, riding him right over the edge of his climax.

His cock still throbbing between my slick walls, Eric sagged beneath me. Reality was an alien thing as I heard my coworkers settling into their seats.

When I caught the sound of the water cooler gurgling, I gave Eric a little shake.

He opened his eyes, but they had a far-off look to them. "This morning I hated my job," he said, "now I love it. You're a good woman."

I blew out a deep breath and glanced around us. "I have no idea how in the fuck I'm going to get you out of here."

"You want me to try and shimmy out the window?"

"Funny guy." I carefully dismounted him and wobbled as I pulled on my panties. "I'm going to have to sacrifice myself for that fuck we just had. Can you hang in here for fifteen minutes?"

"I'm already running late, so what the hell? What's your plan?"

"Just sit tight, and don't forget your crutch out front."

Twenty minutes later, I had the entire staff gathered in the break room after a coffee and cheesecake run to the delicatessen in the lobby and handed out the treats to give Eric the opportunity to disappear unnoticed.

As soon as I was sure he was gone, I lost all interest in being the social coworker and returned to my office. The receipt for the water was on my chair and there was a folded piece of paper on my keyboard.

> *You forgot to sign my cast. Took your cell number from your phone, hope you don't mind. Pizza at my place tonight? Need more TLC later. Also, lots of sex. Eric.*

I love Fridays.

CALIFORNIA DREAMIN'

Andrea Dale

I looked out my home office window at our pool, glittering blue in the Southern California sunshine, and thought, *It's just not fair.*

I know, I know—how selfish and prima donna-ish does that make me sound? I work at home, and I have a *pool*, and I'm whining. First-world problems and all that.

In truth, I have little to whine about, and I'm honestly grateful. Trent, my husband, has a fantastic job with a film production company, which allowed us to move to L.A. and allowed me to work at home on my screenplays. Yeah, his job takes him overseas for a few weeks at a time, and I whine about that, but absence makes the heart grow fonder.

Or in our case, makes the loins grow needier. Our reunions are really, *really* good. Put it this way: the neighbors called the cops one time because of my screaming. I call that a win.

We joked that we'd become a typical California couple: we had Hollywood jobs, we were nominally open in our relationship and we had a pool complete with a pool guy.

And there was the problem.

Our pool guy was not the clichéd tanned, ripped stud muffin with sun-kissed shaggy blond hair that the movies had promised me. Oh, no.

Our pool guy was a grizzled older man, wiry, his face prematurely wrinkled and spotted from the sun. I'm not saying he was hideous, just that he wasn't my cup of tea—especially because he smoked.

I managed to convince Joe not to smoke while he cleaned our pool, largely because my office window opened onto the pool, and he'd agreed. He was a good guy, albeit taciturn. We had our routine: I left the back gate unlocked on cleaning days; he arrived, cleaned our pool, and stuck the bill in the mailbox; I locked the back gate behind him. The end.

And then one day I looked out my office window, thinking *It's not fair* because it was pool-cleaning day and I didn't have a pool-cleaning Adonis to look forward to, when there she was.

A pool-cleaning Aphrodite.

She was blonde, and gently tanned, and lithe. Were she a cliché, I supposed she'd be wearing a teeny bikini. Instead, she wore a cute little pair of shorts (hey, it was a hot, sunny day), a faded T-shirt with the sleeves ripped off and an enormous straw hat to protect her from the sun. As I watched, she slathered her arms and legs with sunscreen—in an efficient way rather than a deliberately sexy way, although my breath stuck in my throat and my groin went heavy with need—before picking up the pool skimmer.

I retained enough presence of mind to realize I should find out who the stranger in my backyard might be. I retained enough vanity to change out of my jammies, put on a bra, fluff up my hair and swipe on some gloss. Hey, had I gone for full-on makeup, I'd have been a cliché myself.

I didn't want to look like a Real Housewife.

I didn't want to look obvious.

I didn't consciously process at least one of those things.

In an effort not to startle her, I heaved on the sliding glass door with more effort than usual, letting the bang when it opened alert her to my presence.

She turned, smiled. Oh, thank goodness, she really wasn't a Hollywood cliché. Perfectionism is *boring*. She had a slight overbite (which made me want to suck on her upper lip) and small, unenhanced breasts (unlike me, she didn't need to wear a bra, mmm) and curvy hips (okay, I'd noticed those before) to go along with her athletic thighs.

"Hi," I said. "I'm Annette. The homeowner." I stuck out my hand.

"Oh, hi!" she said, closing my fingers in a firm grip. "I'm Star. I'm—Joe's my dad."

"Is he okay?"

"Yeah, mostly. He's having a hip replacement." Star leaned casually on the pool skimmer. "He's been talking about passing on the business, so I've been taking on more of his jobs. I hope that's not a problem."

"Not at all," I said, in a way that I hoped wasn't at all lascivious.

"He said you mostly kept to yourself, so I just let myself in."

"Actually, it was your dad who never seemed to want conversation," I said.

She threw back her head, her laugh hearty and unselfconscious. "That's Dad for you. Get in, do the job, get out."

"Like bad sex," I said before I could stop myself. But Star laughed even longer and heartier, long enough that I could admire the length of her neck and fantasize about sucking a hickey there while she moaned and shifted restlessly beneath me.

Bisexual cliché that I am.

"Well," she said finally, "Dad and I aren't much alike. I'm all about getting to know people and doing the job right."

Was she flirting with me? Was I just projecting things? My head whirled. *I didn't know.*

I left her to her job, though...and when she was done, I was waiting with an icy glass of lemonade.

This all happened in the first week of one of Trent's trips, a particularly long one of six weeks. Pool cleaning happened once a week, and by week three, we had progressed to a shared pitcher of lemonade (I was the last house on her rounds) and I knew her full name was Starshine (Joe, it turned out, was a closet hippie) and that she liked '70s prog rock (again, her dad), had a master's in business and brewed her own beer.

We were sharing one of those beers on week four, out-nerding each other with movie quotes, although she was winning because I was kind of distracted by her cute little overbite, when she stopped suddenly and said, "You know, Annette, I'm really glad I met you. I've been so busy running the business with Dad that I don't get out much, and most of my clients end up having lecherous husbands who would rather leer at me than find out I have a brain."

I know I flushed. I clinked the neck of my bottle against the one she was holding out, and before I could stop myself (I blame the afternoon alcohol), I said, "What about the lecherous, leering wives?"

Star laughed and said, "Oh, I have those, too. They—" and just as I decided to fling myself into the pool and drown myself in my embarrassment, she gasped, "Oh, Annette, not *you*! You're not lecherous at all! You..." She bit her lip, looking down in an adorable mixture of cute and coy. "You don't leer." She looked back up at me. "You *admire*."

"Well," I said when I got my voice back, gesturing with my beer, "what's not to admire?"

She leaned forward, her elbows on her knees. "Why Annette, are you flirting with me?"

I leaned forward as well. Our faces were quite close. "It depends on whether you want me to be."

She cocked her head. "You're married."

So I explained the arrangement that Trent and I had. How we could have flings, as it were, with prearranged discussion and agreement.

Star pondered that. "Have you told him about me?" she asked.

"I haven't," I admitted. "Until now, you've been...just a fantasy. I guess I wanted to keep that fantasy between me and my vibrator until he got home. I didn't...want to get my hopes up, you know?"

She laughed softly, her breath scented with hoppy beer. There was a sheen of sweat on her nose. "Oh, I know," she said, in a tone that made it very clear that she'd been having similar naughty thoughts.

My stomach tightened and my pussy clenched.

As first kisses go, it might have been slow, but it was anything but sweet or tender. There were teeth involved, gently tugging (my fantasy about her upper lip, and apparently her fantasy about my lower lip), and tongues, and it went on for what seemed like forever (ugh, cliché), and my head was swimming by the time we pulled apart.

"Are you going to tell your husband about me now?" she asked.

"Oh, *hell* yes!"

* * *

All I had to say was "Hot new pool girl," and Trent was all "Jesus fucking Christ, *yes,* as long as you tell me all about it in excruciating detail afterward."

I did him one better. After talking about it with Star, who agreed enthusiastically, I simply Skyped Trent and set up the laptop before Star and I went after each other like lust-crazed, vampire, shape-shifting zombies (or whatever it is the moms pretend their teens are into these days for an excuse to be into it themselves).

We weren't putting on a show for Trent, and we all knew it. Star and I wanted each other—badly—and after one brief moment of wondering how much Trent could actually see (I imagined it was a flash of naked thigh here, the sweet curve of the side of a breast there and other random body parts), I concentrated on the luscious delights before me.

We dove right into some enthusiastic kissing, with all the nibbling that the previous encounter had entailed, but this wasn't slow or exploratory. This was drinking each other up, tongues dancing and teeth knocking together while our hands roamed restlessly.

Neither of us had dressed up for the encounter, and for me, at least, that added to the deliciousness. I indulged in my fantasy of swirling my tongue behind Star's ear before trailing down to the spot where her neck met her shoulder and branding her with my teeth and lips. Then I helped her peel off her T-shirt so I could feast on her small, unfettered breasts.

She gave a throaty moan when I fastened on to one rosy, plump nipple, and the sound sent electric shocks down to my groin. My own nipples hardened in response, and her wandering hands found them and pinched. Not enough pressure thanks to my shirt and bra being in the way, but enough to make me squirm and suckle her harder.

It's always a delight to discover what a new lover likes. Star's breasts were sensitive—not too much pressure for her, but when I got it right, her hips started a grinding dance beneath me.

So I slid those little shorts right down her lightly tanned legs, pausing only long enough to admire her cute purple thong before tugging it off as well.

"You're overdressed," she murmured, reaching for me. We sat up long enough to divest me of my clothes, and then I found myself on my back while she feasted on my finally, blissfully free breasts. Her teeth scraped against my sensitive flesh and a steady, pounding rhythm started in my clit.

I reached down beneath my legs—no surprise to find myself drenched—and reached back up to coat my nipples and give her a taste. She sucked my fingers and my breasts together, pausing only to squeal when I found my way between her legs, through the trimmed blonde curls, to dip in and learn what she tasted like.

Summer and sunshine and a tartness like oranges.

I wanted more.

I knelt between her legs and danced my tongue around her fat clit, while she wound her hands in my hair and throatily gave me gasped praise. "God—yes—circles—oh, that's perfect—yes—"

I pushed two fingers inside her tight, wet warmth, wishing I'd thought to buy a new dildo, and then forgetting that wish when my fingers proved to be enough. There's nothing like the feel of a woman's pussy pulsing against your fingers as she comes.

My own cunt shivered in response, empathy shivers, not quite an orgasm.

She didn't make me wait long, though. She paused to flick her tongue at my navel ring and discover that made my hips buck.

My clit hummed with need the closer she got to it. Then it was her turn between my thighs, and I'm not a talker when it comes to that. I urged her on with increased panting and moaning, not able to stop even if I'd wanted to, as she drove me closer and closer to release.

I closed my eyes, focusing on the feel of her very talented tongue against my very needy clit and her fingers inside me, and I vaguely remembered she had small hands, and holy mother of—how many fingers was that?—and I went off like a rocket.

When you're coming, you don't worry about clichés.

She slid up my body, a grin on her face, her lips and chin sheened with my juices. What was a girl to do but lick them off? And then we were kissing again, and rubbing against each other, and at some point I know I screamed.

It's a good thing the neighbors know what not to do when they hear me scream. If the police showed up, it would be a like a bad porno.

Also at some point, we discovered my laptop had died because I'd forgotten to plug it in.

Star and I laughed and laughed. "Poor Trent," I said. "I wonder how much he got to see?"

As if in answer, my phone chimed to let me know I had a text:

Aaaaargh! I love you! Call me if you ever finish.

"I think I heard it first ding an hour ago," Star said.

Which got us laughing again, of course.

To cool off, we went out and dove into the pool, of course. We have a private backyard, walls and greenery shielding us from prying eyes, and Trent and I never wear suits unless we have company.

What they say about cold showers doesn't extend to cool pools. We did swim a bit, yes, but somehow I found myself on the shallow steps, Star's hands on my ass and my hips in the air so she could taste me again. It was all I could do to keep my head above water.

And then we repaired to the hot tub, where I turned on the jets and turned her to face them, pressing my lips to the mole on her shoulder. My fingers traced and tickled her wonderfully sensitive nipples while the water spurted over her clit until she shuddered and came again.

By contrast, when we showered the chlorine off ourselves, we were almost sedate.

Almost.

Dried off and dressed, we kissed good-bye. She had to go home and let her dog out; I had ten pages to write before I could call my workday over.

"My legs are so weak, I'm not sure I can drive," she said with a laugh. "Damn, that was a workout. I'm glad I have tomorrow off."

"But you'll be here Thursday to clean the pool…"

She kissed me on my nose. "Of course."

She turned back before I closed the door, winked, and added, "I'm looking forward to meeting Trent next week, too."

Bow-chicka-wow-wow.

With a grin, I went inside to call my husband and tell him all about the pool girl in excruciating detail.

Sometimes, life is not just fair, it's pretty damn good.

RULE OF
THUMB

Laila Blake

My eyes moved from the glittering display of a mobile phone company to the life-size pictures of half-naked orange women in the covered-up windows of a tanning salon. The shop between them did not only look out of place—it was hardly visible at all: a relic from a different time, a different cultural attention span. The small window displayed old folios with cracked spines and yellowed pages, next to them restored versions of the same, crisp and beautiful. A sign read: Book-binding and restoration. Graham Winter. A telephone number and scanty open hours were nestled in tiny writing at the bottom. Customers not welcome, apparently. Even the font felt outdated—and not in a way that would send art and design students into paroxysms of vintage typography joy.

I would be lying if I didn't admit to a degree of apprehension. The carefully designed deterring mechanisms were working and for a moment, I considered finding my way back to my car. There had to be other bookbinders not too far away—a short

Internet search had never let me down in this regard. On the other hand, I felt a hint of spite swelling in my chest. Graham Winter had thrown down his grim gauntlet and I wanted to pick it up and hand it back to him with a smile on my face.

I clutched my handbag closer to my chest and pushed the door open. It creaked, and a jingle of tiny brass bells announced my arrival in the small, dimly lit customer area. It featured a dark wooden counter that had seen better days and an old-fashioned chandelier to the side. It wasn't lit. There were little notes spread over the counter and tacked to a board behind it and I turned around to see if this was all. I finally spied a lonely little display case full of artistically bound diaries—and I found myself wondering when they had been touched last. A month ago? Or probably longer?

I stepped closer to the counter, running my fingers over the polished wood. Coughing a little, I tried to announce my presence to whoever was walking around in the next room. I could hear the footsteps creaking on floorboards, but I wasn't sure the same was true for him. I coughed again. Louder.

An old folio lay there, just a few inches to the side. Its spine was ripped away and missing but the hard leather cover was intricate and beautiful, with a few remaining hints of gold leaf ornaments around the illegible title. Carefully, I traced the unfamiliar word with my fingertips—was it a different language? Greek maybe?

"Please don't touch that."

The voice had appeared suddenly and bodiless. Where I had heard the man move around in the other room, I hadn't been aware of his approach at all and my hand snapped back like a chided schoolgirl's.

"Sorry..." I mumbled, momentarily annoyed that I was the one apologizing. He was tall, his brown hair graying around his temples and lines carefully etched into his features. Typical worry lines, I supposed, or lines of concentration: the deep vertical gashes above the root of his nose, the horizontal meridian lines on his forehead. Despite them, he was not unattractive—if intimidating. His eyes—they looked green in the gloom—were bright, expressive and intelligent and I found myself immediately evaluated by his gaze.

"I...would like to get a book bound?" I finally asked when instead of greeting me, he walked around to his side of the counter, gave me a short and vaguely questioning look and then concentrated on picking up the book. He could have done with a customer service handbook, I supposed, but I could see how his method had its merits: he retained all the power.

He didn't answer immediately, handling the folio with infinite patience as he set it down on a protective piece of cloth and folded it over the cover. It was effectively pulled from my reach.

"What kind of book?" he finally asked when he looked up at me again.

"It's not really a book yet, per se." I fumbled around in my bag to unearth a plastic file. I pulled its contents—a good number of old and yellowed notebooks—out and onto the table and shrugged. "I found these among my grandmother's things. Her mother was a poet—she also...she did these drawings." I wasn't sure why I felt nervous as I thumbed through the topmost notebook until I found a blurry pastel watercolor of a robin with tenderly etched childlike features.

"Family memories?" he asked and I wondered if that was derision I heard in his voice. Maybe.

"Something like that. I'd just like to have them all in one place—safe, you know. It would mean a lot to her."

I was rambling, I knew that much. He made me feel uncomfortable and I was only slowly finding my grip again.

He only nodded though, and picked up the notebooks, leafing through them silently. He had the air of a judge or a bouncer—as though if her poems weren't dressed in beautiful enough words, he wouldn't let them anywhere near his precious bindings. I rolled my shoulders to show annoyance, but I had a feeling he didn't see it. Finally, he concluded his analysis with a shrug and then nodded to the back room.

"You will want to choose a binding, I assume?"

"I...yeah sure," I answered, following him. There was that moment of hesitation again as though the building might swallow me whole if I ventured any farther inside of it.

Where the counter had smelled dusty and old, like a room that wasn't lived in and rarely cleaned, the one we entered then was abundant with living smells. Paper everywhere, metals, heat, glue. I closed my eyes to let it soak in. When he coughed though, I blushed and looked at him standing by the enormous work-table. It was heavy and darkened wood, filled with a myriad of notches and other signs of use. Could one man deliver such a tapestry, such a story of craftsmanship into a table like this or had he taken it over from a previous owner?

"The obvious choice is leather," he said in his oddly melodic and yet clipped speech. He pulled out a drawer and handed me a heavy sheet to touch. "These keep books safe. Others are softer to the touch."

I let my fingers glide over the material and tried not to remind myself that it had once been skin. It smelled like my high school boyfriend's jacket and I couldn't help the nostalgic smile on my face.

"How much did you plan on spending? If the budget permits it"—this time I was sure of his sneer—"we could consider leather engravings and gold leaf titles."

I let my eyes wander to the flimsy bits of gold still sticking to a machine next to him and found myself shrugging. I still didn't know what only the simple edition cost but something about him made me afraid to ask. I wasn't used to feeling shy like this.

Trying to appear to be pondering this question, I walked around the room, looking at his tools. He was a Luddite, clearly, preferring old craftsmen's items over new technology. It took me a while to find the mp3 player in a dusty docking station on a shelf. It looked as out of place there as I was bound to look here in the shop.

On a console before me was another book, books everywhere: a bible, this time, black and opened to reveal a beautiful woodcut. I only realized I was reaching out to touch it when a sudden sharp pain on my knuckles caused me to pull my hand back and whirl around. There he was, suddenly so much closer, a long springy ruler in his hand.

"I said no touching." His reminder was spoken clearly and calmly, and while I knew my face was suddenly red hot, he looked as relaxed as ever. There was a pulling sensation between my legs, and I sucked my bottom lip between my teeth. *Fuck.*

"S-sorry..." I whispered and before I knew it, I was smiling up at him. "Sir."

If I was hoping to surprise him, I failed. He just offered a crooked smile in return, calloused and strong fingers running along the sharp edge of the ruler.

I watched them and found myself quite faint at the sight. Before my cheeks exploded, I swallowed and turned around again. My hands on the rough wooden counter, I breathed and counted to five. Had he moved? I had absolutely no idea. Finally, I reached for the book again—a challenge, his move to make now.

I only got halfway there before the crack of the ruler stopped me again. Harder this time, hard enough to make me wince and shudder. I knew I was breathing more rapidly, too. I couldn't turn around, couldn't look at him—not with the way my clit was suddenly pulsing in response—but then he spoke again and I realized I didn't have to turn around at all.

"Bad girl," he rasped, leaning over to brush the bristles of his stubble over my ear. "Keep your hands on the console. Spread your fingers...wider. Good."

Were I to examine the course of events, I might have come to the conclusion that the best decision I could have made would have been to turn around and leave the shop right then—but I neither examined, nor left. Instead I breathed and followed his instructions. He didn't touch me, and I still didn't know exactly where he was standing.

"Close your eyes."

They fell shut before I could protest. The flash of fear mingled with the excitement to interesting effects: the soft, rhythmical contractions of my left thigh; sweat in the small of my back; a tiny shivering whimper that sneaked past my lips. The smells were even more overwhelming now, but this time, instead of paper, I smelled the leather more—leather and old wood.

A sudden flash of pain across my knuckles made me exhale a curse. I pulled my hand away, cradling it in the other. Tears pooled in my eyes but my clit was thrumming, too.

"Did I tell you to lift your hands from the counter?" he asked in his maddeningly calm voice—maddening because it was so warm, so simple, so perfect.

I shook my head.

"I can't hear you."

"No...no, Sir."

"Good girl. Put them back."

I did so, and just for a moment, I eyed my knuckles as though expecting them to be raw and bloody. But they looked nothing more than slightly pinkish, and I felt silly for pulling away like that.

"Eyes closed," he reminded me, with more of a growl this time. I should have remembered this on my own; that much was evident in his voice and in the shameful flush across my cheeks.

"Why are you being punished?" he asked then. I shuddered as he brought the ruler to the side of my face and used its sharp edge to brush the hair away from my cheek and behind my back. It was distracting enough to make me fumble the answer.

"Book," I almost coughed out, "I t-touched your book, Sir."

"No." As though for emphasis, he cracked his ruler over the back of my abused hand again. I whined—louder, kept my mouth closed to avoid the *fuck!* I wanted to utter. Instead I drew the sound out until the last bits of air left my throat with a low groan. I didn't take my hands off the counter.

"Be... Because I tried to touch it when you said not to touch it," I tried again. No crack this time. The relief made me almost dizzy—or was that disappointment?

"Why did you try to touch it?" he asked. I could hear he smirk in his voice.

"I..." I knew the answer, but it was hard to say. I hesitated only a second or so, maybe three, but the ruler found its mark again with agonizing precision—never the fleshy part of the back of my hand, always the sensitive, bony knuckles. I think I wailed out loud this time. "Because you...because you smacked my hand!"

"Good girl..."

I don't think I could feel my head in that moment—an empty

floating thing, utterly happy to be led around like a helium balloon on a string. Finally, I could feel his hands, too. He was running two fingers down my spine, easily traceable under my tight sweater. When he reached the small of my back, I curved my spine inward, pushing out my rear, and I could feel more pressure resting on my hands.

"Eager..." he whispered, smiling, and took his hand away. Now I definitely wanted to cry. I don't know how evident this was on my face but it had to have been visible because he tutted instantly. "Punishment first, young lady."

I think I came a little bit right then and there.

"Don't move," he instructed again and this time, I did hear him move away. There was that temptation to see where he was going, what he was fetching, or just to remind myself what he looked like again. My head was foggy now with the vaguest recollection of clear green eyes and graying hair, a lack that was not quite fitting the physical and emotional response I was suddenly having toward him. I didn't move though. Maybe I wanted to prove I could do as I was told; maybe I just didn't know how to disobey him anymore.

When he came back, he stopped next to me. For a few seconds, nothing happened and my breathing accelerated nervously. Was he watching me?

Suddenly, a soft band was placed over my eyes. My lips formed a protest I didn't utter but I stiffened slightly, swallowing hard. I could smell it now, soft buck leather, and he was tying it at the back of my head. I wondered if I was still standing straight or swaying on the spot, genuinely unable to tell.

"Turn around," he instructed then, and I lifted my hands from the relative safety of the counter. It was harder than I thought—blindly turning. In the end, he stopped me before I moved too far. It was just a hand on my arm, pressing softly, pulling me back—but it went in little shivers all through my body.

"Hold out your palms, higher, farther out. Farther. Good girl."

I was just able to lean my rear against the counter but my hands were stretched out far in front of me now—far enough to hurt a little without him doing the slightest thing. Panicking slightly, I wondered how long I would be able to keep them there and whether he would stop if I let them fall or even just sink a few inches. I wanted to see him, I wanted to touch him, I wanted his cock in my mouth and I wanted to stand right there, stomach in knots and wondering what he would do next.

Why, why is fear so intoxicating?

Just when I thought I couldn't take it anymore, he made his move. I heard the swish a fraction of a second before the ruler connected with my palms. A loud smack, a grunt of pain, a dark and desperate twinge in my clit. But however fervently I tried, I couldn't push my legs together hard enough to press against it and relieve just a hint of that pent-up need.

"Up," was all he said, and the moment I lifted my hands to their original position, the same crack, the same smacking strike. I think I cried out this time, but so many of these moments are a blur now. He started smacking faster, harder, and I cried into the buck leather until I begged him to fuck me, begged him to stop, begged him to touch me just a little bit before I might implode.

I hadn't realized it at first but I had slumped forward far enough to press my temple into his chest, breathing hard and trying to recuperate. He too smelled like leather; leather, old paper and expensive coffee beans.

"Shhh..." he whispered, fingers cradling my head, curling in my hair and behind my ears. I could feel the small caresses, petting me and giving me time. I tried not to think about what a shaking, crying, sweating mess I was becoming.

"What do you say?" he finally whispered. Again his lips were so close to my ear, I could hear each plosive sound as a tiny click reaching deep into my conscience.

"Thank you..." I breathed without thinking, "Thank you, Sir."

"Such a good girl." He held me a little longer until I nosed and gingerly pawed at his chest. "I want you on your knees, little girl."

And onto my knees I sank. The ground was hard wood but I didn't wince, neither did I moan when he took my hands and rubbed his rough thumb into my sore palms.

I heard the sound of his fly, then the dull snap of old elastic and finally, he brought my hands to his cock. It was glorious, warm and hard—the skin so soft at the same time. Letting my fingertips wander carefully, I explored his length and girth; I found the beautiful distinction between its head and the shaft and finally traveled down all the way to his ball sac.

"Take it in your hand," he said then. There was something about the grumbling, growling quality of his voice that was like warm thunder. "Really take it in your hand."

I tried, hardly feeling his skin against the sore numbness of my palms and fingers.

"Harder."

I whimpered, swallowed hard and then found my stride, pumping up and down his shaft as he guided the direction. With the darkness surrounding me under his blindfold, each sensation seemed multiplied, echoing across my sensory landscape: my aching fingers, his steadying hand, the tiny grunts from somewhere above. My own clit seemed ready to burst, but I didn't quite dare to plead with him anymore. Finally, oh, finally his hand found the back of my head and pulled me forward. My mouth opened without prompting and he used his cock as a brush to paint a stroke of precome over my bottom lip. Warm shudders danced down my spine.

"Good girl," he growled again and already, my chest seemed to swell with pride at the compliment.

His finger on my chin, he pulled my jaws even farther apart and finally let his cock enter. It didn't feel like a blow job, it felt like a ceremony of claiming. My mouth was now his and when his grip tightened in the back of my neck, my throat was delivered into his property as well, spluttering and choking. And in trade, he gave me wings or a hot-air balloon and I was flying feet from the ground, moaning softly around his cock as he pushed it against my gag reflex over and over.

My fingers pawed at his trousers, at his belt—sore as they were, I couldn't stop the desperate need to touch him. I hardly remembered his face at all now; he had become a voice, a cock, a pair of hands, incorporeal and immensely powerful—and I was kneeling at his feet.

"When I come," he said then, voice straining just a little away from the calm and powerful air he exuded and turning to a growl, "you will feel the need to swallow, little girl. But I want you to keep it on your tongue. Do you understand? Keep it. Keep it and show me."

I could feel it then, the little tremors and shivers that went through his cock, the way he wanted to dance and wriggle in my mouth but was forced over and over into a wet tunnel too narrow to do much of either. In this heightened, desperate state, I could even feel his seed, pumped through his shaft a second before it sprayed into my waiting, hungry mouth. And I resisted the urge to drink it down. The sharp taste burned on my tongue; it sent my body into wild shudders, but I kept it there anyway.

"Good girl," he said again, and pulled out and touched the side of my face so gently. "Show me."

On his command, my mouth fell open to display the viscous liquid pooling on my tongue, and he patted my cheek.

"Good. Good. You may swallow once you're back in your car, little one."

Panic, red hot and burning, shot through me. I whined, unable to beg him with a mouthful of come, unable to show him my need in any other way with my eyes hidden behind his soft leather blindfold. He chuckled, and I whimpered again, desperately rubbing my cheek against his hand like a pet, like a kitten begging for attention. *Don't send me away, please, please don't send me away!*

"You may come back tomorrow to choose a binding." Once more he petted my cheek and then bodily lifted me to my feet and led me back to the front area. "Oh, and if you really have to touch yourself—nothing but your hand. Understood? I want you to feel your punishment."

I nodded. "Y-yes...Sir." My head swung around once or twice trying to catch my bearings in the darkness.

Then suddenly, the blindfold was lifted, his hand moved away and a door closed behind me before I could turn around to him. I was standing there, blinking at the display case full of beautifully bound diaries, his come in my mouth and my clit throbbing.

I noticed my bag at the side of the door, and, as in trance, I reached for it. I put my phone on the floor next to it—I would come to collect it the next day.

KNEADING LESSONS

Tilly Hunter

I'd smiled at the line of flour crossing the pockets of Tom's jeans as I followed him into the back of the bakery. He had a firm ass, but I couldn't decide if the soft denims were super-expensive or just hadn't been washed for a month. I'd been flirting with him over the counter for weeks. Ever since I'd first seen that program with celebrity chef Joel Watson that had enlightened me on the horrors of factory-made bread.

I'd gone on a quest for a decent bakery and found Tom's quaint little shop just outside the ring road. Wild-haired, thick-armed Joel had merged in my fantasies with shaven-headed Tom's sparkly eyes and cheeky grin. I suspect it was the shared Scottish accent, all soft and rounded with that oh-so-correct pronunciation of all the *wh* words. All I could think about at night was a deep voice whispering oh so correctly in my ear as strong hands kneaded my flesh.

Now I had a momentary reality check. Within minutes of arriving on the pretext of getting some baking tips from this virtual stranger, I was lying naked on his table, my back and butt grinding into flour and grain and crumbs of dough, legs open and cunt on display. And it felt so good.

Single for over a year, I'd nurtured my new obsession with real bread as the latest substitute for sex. Joel had captivated me from the TV screen as he kneaded a floury lump until it responded like a live being in his hands, turning soft and silky and smooth. I'd always had a thing for men's forearms and Joel's were well muscled and covered in dense, golden hair that ended up tangled with specks of dough. His talk of wild yeasts and stone-ground rye and hand-pressed virgin olive oil was an enchantment. But right now I wasn't thinking of Joel's firm grip on my butt but that of Tom, not a celebrity chef but a real master baker with real strong fingers.

I'd gone to his bakery for help, after yet another disaster that morning. As I'd lifted my hands from the worktop, the dough clung to them and I already feared the worst. It slowly peeled from my fingers and hit the lightly floured surface with a thud.

"Wetter is better," said the recipe from Joel's book. Chance would be a fine thing, I thought. After precisely ten minutes of stretching and pummeling, I dropped the gooey mess into a bowl, covered it with plastic wrap and placed it in the airing cupboard, where my thermometer confirmed the correct temperature of eighty degrees Fahrenheit.

I'd spent the next two hours on a report for work, having long since forgotten my rule of never working on a Sunday, now that I had no significant other to distract me. Sure enough, the dough had risen in its allotted time, although I was finding it hard to judge by eye exactly what "doubled in size" meant. I thought about Joel Watson's cock doubling in size when it was kneaded and warmed.

As I'd set to shaping the dough, the doorbell rang and I

placed a floury fingertip on the intercom. "Hello?"

"Hi, Emma, it's Paula. Do you want to come out for lunch?"

"I'm a bit busy, but come up and have a cuppa."

I buzzed Paula, my colleague and closest friend, into the building and knocked the latch off the door with my elbow.

"What the hell are you doing?" Paula asked, looking at my hands.

"Making bread."

"Why?"

I wouldn't expect Paula to understand. We'd eaten many a takeaway together. Paula admitted she'd never used her cooker, only the microwave for frozen ready meals. But for me, Joel's show and book had been a revelation and I'd vowed never to touch a plastic-wrapped, presliced lump of cotton-wool white again. Instead, Tom's bakery had introduced me to chewy-crusted Campagne, dense and nutty rye bread, flaky, butter-rich pastries and tongue-tinglingly sweet sponge with dark candied cherries on top.

"I saw this TV program with a guy called Joel Watson about how bad the industrial bread-making process is for you," I said. "That's why so many people are becoming allergic. The process is too fast. So I thought I'd make my own."

"Joel who?" said Paula. "A slice of toast never made me ill. I'll put the kettle on."

I'd carried on shaping, flattening, folding, rolling. I placed the dough in the tin, seam side down, and returned it to the airing cupboard.

"So are you too busy for lunch, then?" Paula asked. "I fancied the Royal Oak. They do a very nice steak baguette."

"Yeah, semi-baked in a factory and delivered frozen to be finished off in five minutes in their chemically cleaned ovens.

I've got to wait for this dough to prove. Why don't you stick around and try it?"

"It'd better be good," Paula said. "Why don't you get a machine?"

"It wouldn't be the same. Bread's one of the simple basics of life; I want to be able to do it myself." *And I have nothing else firm and organic and wholesome to get my hands on*, I thought.

"You've lost me already. That new trainee starts tomorrow," Paula went on. "I heard he's a bit older than usual. You could be in there. He's tall too, apparently."

"I'm not that old," I complained. "And I don't like lanky blokes." I couldn't talk to Paula about the kind of men I liked; she was no good at being discreet.

"You'll never get anyone with that attitude. My Mikey isn't exactly the hunk I'd always imagined. You have to compromise once you hit your thirties."

"I've only just turned thirty. And I certainly don't want an office romance." I had particular tastes. I didn't want some suited office clone but a real man who could take charge.

I put the dough in to bake and set the timer, glad when the beeper went off just as Paula was getting into full flow about her boyfriend's flaws.

The bread looked brown enough. It smelt cooked. I tipped it out of the tin, tapped its bottom. It sounded hollow all right, but with a rather deep tone. It still hadn't risen much. I wondered if Joel Watson's bottom had a hollow ring when you tapped it. Or Tom's.

"Isn't it supposed to be bigger than that?" asked Paula.

"I don't know why it won't rise. The only thing I can think of is the yeast. The book says to use a liquid sourdough starter but I couldn't find any so I used dried."

I carved off a couple of steaming slices and slathered them in butter. "Don't you have any low-fat spread?" Paula said. "I've got to watch my weight."

"No, don't you know how bad that stuff is for you? Hydrogenated fats."

"Who cares if you can fit in a size six?"

"Well you're the one talking about steak baguettes."

The loaf was softer than the last one. But chewing it still made my jaw ache. Paula usually spoke her mind, but I could see her trying to put on an appreciative face.

"Don't worry, I know it's awful."

"Steak baguettes it is then?"

"I'm just going to make a call about the yeast. You know that bakery I've been going to. I don't suppose it'll be open on a Sunday, but I'll give it a try." I didn't mention Tom and his warm, twinkly eyes in a face that would be dimple-cute without the skinhead.

"Hello, Village Bakery." That accent.

"Oh hi. I'm Emma, I've been coming in for your Campagne recently. I was wondering whether you sell sourdough yeast starters?" My voice was nervy; I couldn't shake the feeling that Tom might have some mind-reading superpower to see the filthy things my imagination had made him do to me.

"Oh hi, Emma, you're the one who likes the cherry cupcakes, aren't you?" I flushed as I thought about Tom biting my ripe red nipples. "Nice to hear from you. But we don't sell starters, no."

"Oh, well, thanks anyway." I went to hang up.

"No, you don't understand. We don't sell it—we give it away. Don't you know about the old bakers' code?"

"Code? No. I don't know what you mean."

"We're not allowed to sell yeast, some ancient rule. I can

bottle some up for you. What are you baking anyway?"

"Oh, just bread. But not very well. I think it must be the fast-action yeast."

"Probably. Yeast's a living thing, you can't go drying it out and expecting it to work instantly. And there's no such thing as 'just bread.' Look, I'm not open today, but if you come round I'll get you some starter, and I can give you a few tips. Just knock, I'll be in the back trying out new recipes." I couldn't believe I was getting hot just over his voice. I really needed to get laid but had settled for celibacy rather than dull sex on a one-night stand.

"Okay, I'll be there soon."

As I hung up, Paula looked at me suspiciously. "Why have you gone all red?" I pretty much shoved her out of the door.

I knew I was going for more than a few tips. Maybe a swapping of phone numbers, a tentative agreement to meet for a drink. I drove into the countryside trying to rein in my fantasies about my Joel Watson/Tom-the-master-baker fusion. My cheeks had a telling flush by the time I parked and checked them in the rearview mirror.

Tom was wearing a novelty blue apron covered in pictures of pink- and purple-iced cakes. He still managed to look hot, the sort of man who'd make a kids' party hat sexy. The sleeves of his casual white shirt were rolled up. He had more stubble than usual, enhancing his not-really-trying good looks. He was actually quite different from the neat and, if I had to admit it, slightly arrogant Joel Watson. But the impressive forearms were there.

"You look younger in your civvies. Come through to the back. I'm just experimenting with some chili wholegrain for baking tomorrow," he said, holding up floury hands in explanation.

His timings confused me. And had he just insulted me over my age? I followed him. That was when I noticed the dusty line across his backside.

The working area was mostly clinical stainless steel and health-and-safety notices but Tom headed for a well-scrubbed wooden table that wouldn't have looked out of place in a farmhouse kitchen. There was a mound of tan-colored dough on it, spiked with chopped red chili, along with piles of grain-dotted flour and gleaming bottles of oil. The dough was ten times the size of anything I'd worked with.

"Here's your starter. I've put it in a bottle, hopefully it won't leak. Don't want to mess up your nice clean jeans." My pussy clenched at the thought of sticky, white liquid messing up my nice clean jeans. God, I really, really needed to get laid.

"Can I just ask?" I said. "You say you're getting dough ready to bake tomorrow, but my book says it takes two hours to rise and half an hour to prove, so how can you be doing it now?"

"Oh, and I suppose your cookbook's always right, is it?" he said, good-humouredly. "It all depends—on the type of dough, the temperature, the hardness of the flour. Whose book is it?"

"Joel Watson's."

"That fraud? He wouldn't know his baps from his bagels."

I subconsciously stood taller, pushing my chest out, as he mentioned baps. His eyes glanced down. Had he done it on purpose? "Oh, I saw him on TV. He sounded like he knew what he was talking about. And when he kneaded the dough, er, he looked experienced enough."

"He's all show. You can't teach that sort of thing on TV or in a book. You have to get a feel for dough." He flexed his fingers as he spoke and I imagined him taking a breast in each hand. "You can tell when it's soft enough, risen enough, stretchy enough." His voice made me think about my soft pussy, swelling with arousal and stretching around his cock.

"Wow, and I thought I could just follow the recipe. I really want to be able to bake, but my loaves have all been bricks. I wish I had the feel for it, it would have saved me a lot of wasted effort."

"But that's what it's all about. It's a slow process, you have to get to know the dough."

"Sounds like a blind date. Do you have to buy it a drink as well?"

"Only if it's lukewarm tap water. I was just kneading this batch," he said. "You have to be gentle and firm at the same time." My knees went a bit wobbly. I watched him gently stretching the dough away from him, then pulling it back, folding it over. "It doesn't want pummeling. You have a go."

I copied his actions, trying to be gentle but firm, but I couldn't do it as smoothly, as effortlessly as he did and all I could think about was the word *pummeling*. The dough clung to the scrubbed grain of the table. "That's good," he said. "Now fold it back." But he was just being kind.

"You do it," I said. "It's much nicer watching you."

"Well, you'll never learn that way, but all right, for now," Tom said with a smile. He carried on and the dough began to change, to look silky and soft. "That should do it, you can see it's had enough now. We'll give it a rest next to the oven and let it rise."

He set it down in a big earthenware bowl beside a brick structure. "I like this oven best," he said. "But it takes a while to heat up so I keep it lit, in the winter anyway. It warms my flat upstairs."

"Is it wood fired?" I asked. "There's a smoky smell. It's like my mum's wood burner."

"Yes, lovely isn't it? In the autumn I get prunings from

Howarth's orchard and then it smells really sweet." Surely he was too good to be true, not just any old baker but a man who understood wood and fire.

"Well, now we have to leave it," he said, and paused. "So, do you want to buy me a drink? That's if you've no Sunday dinner to get back to." He started washing his hands at the obligatory health-and-safety sanitation station.

I smiled at his cheek. "No, just bread and butter in front of the TV."

"A drink it is then." He pulled off his apron. "A present from my mum," he said, explaining the cakes.

"You've got flour on your..." I began, gesturing toward his backside, "on your jeans."

"Oh?" He tried to look over his shoulder to see. "So have you," he said.

"No I haven't."

"Yes, you have."

"No, I..." As I turned to try to see, brushing my jeans just in case, I felt his arms around me. I looked back at him and he kissed me. Gentle but firm. I leaned against the wooden table.

"You have now," he said.

"Do you want to skip the drink?" I said, bold with arousal. I hardly knew this man.

"I'd like that." He leaned in for another kiss and I grabbed the back of his neck to pull him in harder. Stubble prickled my chin. His warm hands edged under the hem of my jumper and in one big *fuck it* moment I pulled both jumper and T-shirt off, threw them aside and slid out of my bra. His fingers went straight to my nipples, the pads circling and making my spine tremble.

"Just like those cherry cakes you like so much," he murmured, bending his head to take one in his mouth and nip it. "Or are you more of a savory dish?" he said, dipping his fingers in flour and dusting my breasts like soft luncheon rolls. It made his warm hands glide drily over me with just a hint of grit from the coarse grain. I pushed my backside up to sit on the edge of the table, careless of the mess on my jeans. "Yes, more like firm, sharp olives than cherries," he said, easing me back to lie on the wooden surface. I let him undo my belt and zip, lift my butt off the table and slide my jeans and knickers off, my shoes clattering to the tiled floor. I reached down and finished the job by thumbing off my socks before shimmying up so I could get my heels on the edge.

That was when the reality check hit me. "Tom," I said. "I'm really not normally like this. And I don't have any condoms."

"You've been flirting with me for weeks. I was going to pin you down to at least a drink this week anyway. But now you're here. All naked." He ran a finger down between my breasts and over my stomach. "We might as well make the most of it. And I could probably find a condom somewhere in my flat." I wondered if his choice of the words "pin you down" had been intentional. They certainly made my pussy pulse.

"You'd better go and look."

"Don't move," he said, as he disappeared through a back door. My nipples were still tingling. In fact, they were tingling with a hot, itching sensation. Tom was back quickly, holding up a silver packet.

"Tom, my nipples seem to be burning," I said.

He looked confused and then horrified. "Shit, I've been chopping chilies. Oh fuck, I'm sorry."

"It's all right," I said. "I like it. I want to feel it all over."

He raised an eyebrow and reached for my breasts again, kneading them in exactly the way I'd imagined. My pussy swelled like rising dough. "I have some chili oil," he said. "If you'd like a massage."

"Oh yes, please."

He took one of the bottles and glugged bright yellow-green oil into his palm. I held my breath, waiting to feel it on my skin. He started with my breasts, of course, slicking over every inch of them and paying particular attention to my hard nipples. It took a moment for the tingle to begin, the skin to prickle, heat to build. Tom's hands moved down over my belly, squeezing and pressing, stretching and rolling my flesh into glossy smoothness. I realized the heat was not the same all over. On most of my skin it was a pleasant warmth just on the edge of discomfort, but on my nipples it was a hot flame that made me want to rub and scratch.

"Do you like that?" he asked.

"Yes." I wanted to know what it would feel like on the damp, tender membranes of my pussy. "I want it everywhere."

He knew what I meant. He poured more oil and slicked it over my thighs, thumbs gliding in to tease the edge of my labia. Then he stopped teasing and pushed his dripping fingers into my slit. At first there was just the gliding feel of oil lubricating my lips and clit. Then the warmth began. Tom massaged firmly, sliding the tips of his fingers just inside me and back up to my clit. I moaned loudly as the sensation intensified. The burn took hold. I wanted to claw my fingernails against the tender, itching flesh and had to concentrate hard to keep my hands on the table, pressing my fingertips into the grooved wood. I thought of a harsh brush scrubbing every speck of flour and oil off the surface with steaming hot water.

"That's so good," I moaned. "But hot." I lifted a hand. "I want to stop you, but I don't want to stop you."

He took the waving hand and pressed it to the wood. "Lie still and enjoy." He stopped massaging and took my other hand, pressing my wrist into the table, then knelt so his arms were stretched over the edge to mine and pushed his face into my cleft. His warm, wet mouth soothed my swollen, flaming flesh for a moment. But the soothing didn't last. His tongue flicked my clit while my skin burned and my pussy longed for friction to salve the irritation around my entrance.

"Fuck me," I groaned, lifting my head to look at him. "Please fuck me."

"Not until you've come," he said, before pressing his glistening face back between my legs. He circled the flat of his tongue over me, its abrasive surface almost scratching the burn away, but then switched to flicking with the hardened tip in a way that only enflamed me more. My hungry entrance alternately opened and clenched. I fought to keep my heels on the table edge as my thighs tensed. His hands were firm on my wrists. My orgasm built with a burning itch that was nothing to do with the chili. My throat tightened, eyes pressed shut and every muscle of my body tensed. I came with a yell of abandonment, squirting into Tom's face.

Sheer embarrassment overwhelmed me. I rarely squirted and couldn't believe it had happened on the first time with someone. It must have been the added stimulation of the chili. "Sorry," I whispered. "I didn't realize that was going to happen."

"Don't be sorry," Tom said, letting go of my hands and rising, his face obscenely wet. "I loved the feel of it. Although the taste is somewhat overwhelmed by the chili. It's a good job I can handle eating hot stuff. Now I believe you wanted me to fuck you."

He unbuttoned his shirt with agonizing slowness. I wanted him inside me. I squirmed and whimpered. He smiled. It only made me need him more. He shrugged the shirt off and undid his jeans, sliding them off with his boxers, shoes and socks in one move. I got my first view of his body and wasn't disappointed.

Strong but lean. A smattering of chest hair and an endearing line of fluff leading to his pubes. He pumped his semihard cock a couple of times then gasped. "Shit, that burns." It was my turn to smile.

"I know," I said. "Now fuck me."

"Of course." He took out the condom and rolled it over his shaft.

Tom guided his cock to my pussy and rubbed it up and down my slit as it hardened. He slid to my hole and pushed all the way in until I felt his head bump my cervix. The slip-slide of his hard shaft against my burning flesh was like a balm. He fucked me in a firm but controlled way for a while before his breath became ragged and his forehead tightened. I felt him grow bigger inside me moments before he came, grinding his pelvis against me with one hard, shuddering thrust.

The following Sunday morning, I waited for the oven timer to ping. The phone rang and Paula said, "Hi, Emma, how about that lunch we missed last week? I was talking to Mark, the new guy, and he said he might be in the Oak today."

"Sorry Paula, I'm busy baking again."

"Well that's not going to find you a man, is it?"

"Actually, I think I'm going to stop looking for a while."

Paula hung up in bewilderment, and I went back to the kitchen. Tom was slicing the still-warm loaf. He held a piece to my lips and I tore into it hungrily, chili heat spreading over my tongue.

WORK IT OUT

Elisa Sharone

J anuary 1, 2012

Noon

New Year's Resolutions

1. Eat better.

2. Relax more.

3. Travel somewhere amazing.

4. Only buy shoes that really fit, even if the sale price is insane.

5. Meet a nice guy. Or two. Or more.

6. Go to the gym at least two times per week.

7. Try a new workout class.

8. Don't let the laundry pile up.

9. Clean off the desk every Friday afternoon.

10. Keep at least three of these resolutions.

Every year I make a list, and every year I fail to keep even one of the resolutions made in vain. But despite my continued abject failure, each January 1 I pull on my tattered terry-cloth robe, slip on my matted bear-paw slippers, straighten my HAPPY NEW YEAR! tiara, pour a large cup of coffee, pull out my journal and write my list.

Oh, the list. The list always has ten items on it, and the tenth is always to keep at least three of my resolutions. Each year I wonder if that's too many, if my bar is set too high. And each year I remind myself that three isn't such a challenge. That anyone should be able to manage a 30 percent rate of completion. Which, in the grand scheme of things, still amounts to abject failure.

In 2011 I managed to successfully accomplish one of my resolutions. A 33 percent completion rate of the 30 percent goal I'd set actually felt like progress for once! And yet, at the same time, I felt like shit for generally sucking at accomplishing even the smallest of tasks. So this year I've set the bar lower than I ever have before. I will travel somewhere amazing. In all honestly it's not that hard. I will only buy shoes that really fit, because come on, why the fuck do I ever do otherwise? And I should be able to keep the laundry from piling up. Everything else on the list is a stretch goal.

Now, to the gym. May as well sweat out the hangover and get the first gym visit of the week on the books.

xoxo,

Gretch

"Great class, everyone! Good job getting your asses here, and I expect to see you again tomorrow." The cheeriness of the instructor grated on my last nerve. Who has the right to be in such a good fucking mood on the worst-hungover day of the year? And who has a right to look so fucking hot in that tank and shorts?

"You did a good job. Why haven't I seen you in my class before?" he said to my ass as I was bent over stacking my steps and weights. Seriously? Hot instructor man with the tightest ass I'd ever seen was talking to my flabby bottom? Quickly, I straightened up and through my sweat-matted bangs mumbled something about New Year's resolutions and all that.

"I hope to see you back tomorrow. I'm Ben," he said, holding out his hand. My eyes lit on his fingers, long and well-formed, caught a glimpse of the smooth skin of his palm, traveled up his well-muscled forearm popping with veins to his powerful shoulder and finally landed on his soft brown eyes, crinkled with a smile. I meant to just shake his hand and thank him for the ass-kicking workout, but his touch gave me goose bumps and I felt my nipples rise and harden against the tight fabric of my sports bra, and I silently thanked Nike or whatever other goddess had the smarts to pad those things so well.

"I'm Gretchen. Thanks for the righteous ass-kicking. If I can walk tomorrow, I'll see you then." I gave him a wink (where the fuck did that come from?), dropped his hand, and left the classroom. My thighs burned, my arms ached, my abs screamed, but all I could focus on was the wet spot forming between my legs that had nothing to do with the hard workout I'd just subjected myself to.

Home again, I peeled off my gym clothes and the cool air raised gooseflesh, reminding me of Ben's touch in the gym. In the mirror I watched my nipples tighten and flush. Fuck he was hot. Grabbing my favorite glass toy and vibrator, I stretched my aching body out on the bed and ran the cool glass head over the heat of my pussy, smiling at how slick and open I suddenly felt.

I pressed the buzzing silicone to my clit, and my mind drifted to the image of Ben's round, tight ass flexing as he led the step series. My breath grew labored, as though I were back in the classroom, pushing through the pain. My pussy had a mind of its own, its desires sending fantastical thoughts to my brain with each twitch and tingle. And then I was back in the classroom, alone with him, the music pounding...

Ben stood behind me as we switched from the step series to weighted squats. I held the dumbbells on my shoulders, my stance wide, my back straight, and began to sink into the squat.

"Your form is nice but needs a little correction," he whispered into my ear, close enough for me to smell the salt on his skin. He gripped my hips from behind, pressing his fingers into my skin and pulling my ass ever so slightly toward him. As I sank deeper into the squat his hands slipped over my ass to the tops of my thighs, caressing that sensitive spot below the swell of my cheeks. "Feel the hamstring work as you rise back up, tighten your glutes, control the movement," he rasped, his fingers again pressing into my skin, his palms cupping my cheeks as I rose to standing again.

"Again," he said, not moving his hands. I watched us in the mirror as I readjusted my stance and slowly sank into another squat. This time his hands moved to the inside of my thighs, the edges of his fingers grazing my pussy lips through my tight shorts. The backs of his hands pressed against my inner thigh muscles, which quivered with the exertion. "Control on the way up, Gretchen. You must keep your thighs tight as you come back to standing," he whispered, and I felt a bead of sweat roll down my neck and between my breasts.

Slowly, I rose from the squat, and as I did, my thighs pulled his hands together, his fingers squeezing my throbbing cunt lips together between my legs. "Nice, Gretchen, very nice. You have excellent control in your adductors. Excellent strength."

And at that I flexed my thigh muscles, squeezing his fingers tighter against me, my swollen clit pressed tightly between my lips.

"Down again, Gretchen," he commanded, as I relaxed my thighs and again moved into the squat. Ben reached one hand forward, placing his palm on my lower belly, the heel of his hand pressed into my pubis, and he sank to his knees as I went down. His other hand settled between my asscheeks, and he held my pelvis sandwiched between his palms as I pushed my ass into the squat. "Excellent form, G. Your hips are tilted at the perfect angle," he growled up at me. "And push into the floor and up." I moved as directed, bringing my pussy in line with his face. The juices were pooling between my lips, and even I caught a hint of my arousal.

"Let's shift, G. Time for single bent-over rows." He stacked the bench high enough for me to bend over, placing my palms flat on the surface, and placed the weights on either side. "Ten reps, right side."

I shifted back a few steps and lifted the weight. My face was so close to my cunt that I could almost taste the tart saltiness of my come. I lowered and lifted the weight as Ben steadied my hips from behind. "Isolate the lats, control the weight," he said, running one hand up from my hips to my shoulder blade under my Lycra top, pressing the heat of his hand into my slick skin. I lowered the weight, inhaling slowly, measuring my breathing. I felt the clenches in my pussy as I did so, my arousal rising with each breath.

"Concentrate on your pecs, they're doing some of the work," he whispered, his hands slipping around to my chest, his fingers working their way under the strap of my sports bra. His hips pressed into mine and I felt the thickness of his cock between my cheeks. I raised the weight, exhaling sharply as his hands moved over my breasts, catching my nipples between his fingers. "And lower, G. Good set."

But he didn't move his hands, and he pressed his cock harder into my ass. I began to move against him, my hands flat on the bench, circling my hips against his, grinding against his hardness. His hands pushed my bra up, freeing my tits from their strapped-down prison, his palms hot on my skin, my nipples caught tightly between his strong fingers.

"Good work, Gretchen. Let's stretch your abs." And with that he lifted me up to standing and pulled me back against him, watching my reaction in the mirror as he pressed his palms hard against my breasts. My head rolled back onto the hard planes of his chest as I arched my back, pushing my ass harder against his crotch, feeling the pull in my lower abs down to my pussy.

"Down on the mat, G. On your back." I slipped down his body to the floor, on my hands and knees, my hard nipples grazing the floor as I lowered down. I pushed out into upward-facing dog, holding it for a moment, and watched Ben's eyes lock on my exposed chest. "On. Your. Back," he growled. Obeying, I lay down and rolled over, my workout top and bra pushed up around my throat and framing my breasts while Ben stood over me, his trainers straddling my legs. His strength and power bore down above me, and he looked like a well-built giant staring down at me. Ben dropped to one knee and lifted my leg, pushing my knee in toward my chest. "This is a great stretch for the glutes, Gretchen. I know you're tight there," he said, easing my thigh closer to my naked breasts. I felt the stretch in my hip as he lifted my ankle and began to straighten my leg. "Now your hamstrings," he continued, leaning into me as he stretched my body.

My leg draped over his shoulder and suddenly it was his

chest pushing against the back of my thigh, and I could feel the outline of his cock brush against my leg through his tight Lycra shorts. He leaned into me, placing his free hand by my head, and ground his pelvis against mine. His swollen head lodged against my pussy, and with each thrust he...

"Ohfuckohfuckohfuckohfuckohfuck!" I screamed, bucking my hips as the power of my orgasm forced the slippery glass from my cunt and I lost my grip on the vibrator that I had smashed into my clit. I squeezed my legs and rolled to and fro, absorbing the contractions that wracked my body, feeling the satin wetness coat my thighs. After a bit my breathing calmed and my body cooled, but my brain remained lit up with the idea of Ben.

January 2, 2012
6:30 a.m.
Goddamn my thighs hurt. I can barely move. That bastard Ben broke me yesterday. (Oh fuck, how I want him to break me!) How the hell am I supposed show up at his class again today? The smell oozing from my pores won't be workout sweat; it'll be the desperation and odor of self-induced sex that still clings to me. Crept into workout clothes. Crept out the door.

7:30 p.m.
Not a word. Not a single fucking word. No "Hi Gretchen, good to see you again." No "Wow, Gretchen, good job getting through another hard class today." No watching my ass as I slowly and carefully stacked my steps and weights. Fuck you, Ben. Fuck you and your perfect tight ass.

10:00 p.m.
I did it again. Only this time I was in the shower with the

nozzle set just right...

I went to the locker room after class ended, stripped, wrapped a towel around me and headed for the steam room. Technically the steam room was coed, but every time I'd been in there it was girls only, and girls only wearing towels. As was often the case, I was the only one, and I stretched out on the heated tiles and felt the warmth sink into my aching muscles and into my bones. I lay there for a while, my mind wandering, until I was brought back to the present moment with the blast of steam that filled the room with its thick fog. I heard the door open, but I couldn't see who came in. Again I closed my eyes and drifted.

I first felt his hand on my ankle, and slowly he moved his fingertips along my steam-soaked skin, grazing the skin of my thigh just at the edge of the towel. My breath caught and I froze, enjoying his touch but shocked and nervous at the advance. My eyes were still closed, but I knew it was Ben. Tracing along the edge of the towel, he tickled the flesh hidden just beneath it, moving across the top of my thigh, ever closer to the heat between my legs. His thigh nudged my legs apart, my left leg swinging off the edge of the hot bench. My eyes squeezed tightly together, I took a deep breath and felt the damp heat of the steam room wash over my open lips.

The flat of his tongue pressed against my labia, and the newness of the sensation prickled goose bumps over my skin, despite the balmy temperature. With slow, deliberate pressure the man I was sure was Ben licked me from my dripping hole to my swollen clit, and I could barely stay still on the slippery surface. I felt his hands wrap around my hips, his fingers locking together and trapping me in a wrestling hold. No matter how I wanted to writhe, I was under his control.

And controlled he was, rhythmically licking and teasing my

folds with the tip of his tongue, tasting my dripping flesh. His tongue dipped into me, teasing my hole, and a moan escaped my lips. Deeper he pressed into me, drinking my juices as I tried to grind against his mouth. But he controlled me, only letting me have what he wanted to give. His deep caress was followed by a teasing flick across my clit, and the sensation sent a jolt through my cunt, tiny throbs echoing through my pelvis.

Another flick, another throb, another squeal, and then he drew my clit between his lips, sucking lightly as the tip of his tongue circled my hard, exposed nub. His slow lazy circles grew more intense, more insistent, until I felt the blossoming warmth that always hit me...

Right as I came with the shower massager licking my clit, I slid down the wet, hot tile wall and let the water pool between my legs as I shook from the intensity of coming.

No class tomorrow. Go for cardio?

xoxo,

Gretch

January 3, 2012
6:30 a.m.
No class with Ben today. I'm taking the day off. Besides, my whole body aches.

12:30
Gorgeous super-on-sale-but-ill-fitting stilettos resisted. One New Year's resolution kept.

6:00 p.m.
Who am I kidding? I'm going to the gym.

7:00 p.m.

No class. No Ben. At least I blasted some calories on the elliptical. And had a nice, but lonesome, steam. And exceeded my
weekly gym requirement by 50 percent! Two New Year's resolutions kept!

10:00 p.m.

Omgomgomgomg he texted me! *It's Ben. Got ur # from gym.
Stay after tmrw.*

11:00 p.m.

Insanely hot fast orgasm, no time for fantasy.

    xoxo,

    Gretch

January 4, 2012

6:30 a.m.

I'm getting the hang of this workout thing.

7:30 p.m.

Hung out with sweaty gorgeous Ben in the juice bar after class;
he had a weird green protein smoothie and I had a faux colada.
A girl needs her post-workout carbs. Chitchatted about not
much, actually, other than classes at the gym and the smoothie
menu. Hmm...but date fixed for tomorrow night and I am so
excited! Realizing it will be the first time we've seen each other
in clothes.

    xoxo,

    Gretch

January 5, 2012

Noon

Fought off urge to buy ill-fitting stilettos rejected during yesterday's shopping trip. I have a date! And stuck to one resolution twice!

7:30 p.m.
Blasted calories on the elliptical again. Gym visit goal exceeded by 100 percent for the week!!

2:00 a.m.
Can. Not. Sleep. I've tried counting sheep, meditative breathing, even reading a boring book. Time to bring out the big guns. No knickers, easy...

He leads me into one of the private workout studios, the windows frosted to keep prying eyes away. He pulls a mat from the storage cabinet and lays it in the middle of the floor. The lights are dim, and he lights a candle. For a moment I think we're going to do a candlelight yoga workout because the soft tones of Tibetan bells echo in the background.

We're in the middle of the gym, but we're a thousand miles from nowhere, and Ben lifts my top and pulls it over my head. I reach forward and do the same to him, my gaze locking on the swell of his pecs and his solid biceps. His fingertips slip into the waistband of my shorts and stretch the elastic over my hips and down my legs. Somehow we're barefoot already. I stand there naked before him, in awe of his strength, but proud of my own natural curves.

I'm not ready to reveal his body completely. I sink down to my knees on the mat, trailing my fingers down his torso, over his waist, along his perfect obliques and around to his ass. I press my hands into his flesh as I press my face into his groin, inhaling his scent and rubbing against his solid cock, still hidden from me through the merest slip of fabric. From behind I tuck my fingers into his shorts and ease them down inch by excruciating inch until he strains against the fabric pulled tightly around him. With a look up to his liquid eyes I free him and wrap my hand around his shaft, pulling the generous head toward my mouth.

He pulls me up, whispers for me to stand. I do as he bids, and his fingers slide between my lips, gliding over my flesh, and first one, then two fingers push inside me. I slide my hand over his cock, squeezing the head and stroking the shaft, running my palm down to his heavy balls and feeling their weight. In the candlelight we explore each other with serious intent and mutual longing. He withdraws his fingers and my pussy aches to be filled. His slippery digits caress my clit and try as I might to remain focused on his stunning erection, I am lost in the feelings erupting between my thighs and sink into his body as I release...

January 6, 2012
6:30 a.m.
Woke up with sticky thighs while using my diary as a pillow and saw an overnight text: *c u @ 7*

7:00 p.m.
I'm off to meet Ben. So far all I know is the fantasy. Let's see if reality can match up.

Progress on New Year's resolutions so far:

1. Pairs of horrible, uncomfortable shoes not bought: two (okay, one, but I resisted twice!)

2. Gym visits: four! Goal exceeded by 100 percent, which counts as keeping two resolutions!

3. New workout classes tried: two! Both led by hot instructor man! Goal exceeded by 100 percent, you know the drill!

4. Nice guys met: one, I think.

5. Relax more: orgasms. Enough said.

Laundry, travel, and eating well will just have to wait. So far it's shaping up to be a very successful year!

xoxo,

Gretch <3

SM, OR HOW I MET MY GIRLFRIEND IN A QUEER THEATER

Giselle Renarde

I figured she'd hate drag queens.

In university, I read a few feminist-lesbian papers that were pretty anti-drag. I can't remember the reasoning anymore. Something about drag performances being reductive and misogynistic, maybe?

Transwomen didn't seem to like drag queens much, either. I didn't read that anywhere. It was just my impression from chatting with other queer people. So that's another reason I figured Lisa wouldn't be impressed by the drag show at Sisters in Sin Queer Theater.

By training and profession, Lisa was a stage manager. People were always asking if she aspired to be an actor. She didn't. Lisa liked the backstage bit, every aspect of it, from lighting to sound to last-minute prop repairs. That's one reason she enjoyed working at Sisters: in such a tiny theater, one person did everything, all the backstage stuff. In a big theater, you'd have had at least one person on lights, someone else doing the sound, even dressers and props managers. Lisa liked to do it all herself.

When I started volunteering at Sisters in Sin, a lot of people asked me that same question about wanting to be an actor. In truth, I only started there to meet other queer people. It's hard, when you're not a bar person. Or a club person. I always felt weird just going up to a stranger and talking to them for no reason. I'm a quiet queer. I volunteered to hand out programs at Sisters because it seemed like easy work, not too much patron interaction. Quiet queer work.

The first time I saw Lisa, my knees buckled so hard I almost fell into a gay man's lap. She whipped from the backstage area, rushed through the audience and disappeared into her dark glass booth at the back of the house. It didn't matter that Lisa dressed all in black or that she moved like a shadow. I spotted her: tall and curvaceous, a full round face, blonde hair pulled into a neat ponytail. She took my breath away.

"You know that's a tranny, right?" another program hander-outer said to me.

My heart nearly stopped. *That word!* I hated that word, and I hated even more that another volunteer, an out-loud and proud lesbian, would speak with such ire about a fellow queer. I didn't know what to say, so I played dumb and asked, "Who?"

"The SM," said the other volunteer.

"SM?" I figured that must either be an insult I'd never heard, or the big blonde was into sadomasochism.

"Stage Manager," the volunteer clarified.

"Oh." I felt stupid for not knowing, but just because I was volunteering in a theater didn't mean I knew anything about the different jobs there.

I wanted to find out her name, which at that point, I didn't know. She was so stunning, even dressed in simple black slacks and a turtleneck. Nothing fancy, except her black velvet scrunchie. I wanted to know everything about her, but I didn't want to hear it from the mean dyke across the aisle.

In truth, I don't remember how I learned Lisa's name. I must have overheard somebody calling her before a show, or afterward when I stuck around to tidy the theater.

Like I said, I was always a quiet queer. It took a few weeks of watching and waiting before I finally worked up the courage to talk to her. To Lisa. I asked her something sensible. I asked, "Can I help you with anything?"

She was onstage at the time. It wasn't a big stage and it wasn't raised too high. Still, Lisa didn't react. She had this look on her face like she was concentrating hard, and I wondered if she didn't want to be interrupted or if she hadn't heard me.

"Can I help you?" I asked again.

Lisa jumped, like she hadn't realized anybody else was in the theater. Her shock made me smile. It was such an intense emotion that it sharpened her features, and when she looked at me, the glowing blue of her eyes pierced my very soul. I know that sounds corny, but it's absolutely true. Cupid's arrow found my heart. Lisa was the girl for me.

"Help with what?" Lisa asked.

Good question. "I don't know. Whatever you're doing."

"Setting the stage for tomorrow's matinee," she said. Since I'd never heard Lisa talk much to anyone else, I figured she was as quiet as me. But maybe she was just waiting for an opening, waiting for someone to take interest. "Oh, you know what you could do, if you wanted? Collect the sherry glasses and we'll take them backstage for a wash."

I felt weird about going backstage, like the actors would yell at me. They didn't have their own individual dressing rooms, just a partially closed-off space with a row of desks and mirrors along the wall. Lisa picked up their costumes off the floor while they chatted and took off their makeup. The two men had their shirts off, and one of the women was in her bra and panties. We were like ghosts to them. We didn't even exist.

"Call time tomorrow is one o'clock," Lisa said, and the actors looked at her in the mirror, nodding their assent.

"Oh, Lisa!" said the woman in the bra. "I almost forgot, the hem of my dress caught on my shoe…"

"I noticed," Lisa said, ushering me and my dishes to the laundry tub in the corner. "Did it rip?"

The actress looked genuinely concerned. "Yeah, it did. Sorry. Can you sew it up before tomorrow?"

"That's my job."

Lisa seemed almost happy about the repair.

I was about to ask her where I could find some dish soap when one of the shirtless men asked, "Who's your little friend?"

You can only stay invisible for so long, I guess.

"She's FOH," Lisa said.

More codes I didn't understand. I told them, "I'm just a volunteer."

The actors surprised me by saying, "That's great," and "Thank you," and "Sisters couldn't survive without people like you." They really seemed to mean it, and that made me feel like a valuable contributor to the theater. I smiled the whole time I washed their sherry glasses.

After every shift, I stuck around and helped Lisa backstage. She started calling me her "official unofficial Assistant SM," which had a nicer ring to it than "FOH." I'd worked up the courage to ask what exactly that stood for, and it was "front of house": ushers, program hander-outers, people who worked with the public.

I'd worked up the courage to ask Lisa a lot of questions, actually. Even some pretty personal stuff. By the time we'd known each other for three or four months, our lives were twining. After work was done, she'd drive me home so I wouldn't have to take the streetcar at night. Around Christmas, I invited her up to see my tree. It was after midnight, but we sat together on my couch, drinking hot chocolate and eating ginger biscuits.

When she set her mug on my coffee table, I knew she wanted me to kiss her. Lisa was kind of transparent that way. I guess we both were. Love is hard to hide.

In that moment, I wasn't thinking about the cruel jabs I'd overheard from other volunteers. I didn't care what Lisa had between her legs. Sure I wondered if she was pre-op, or post-op, or non-op, or something else altogether, but it made no difference. I was totally besotted with her, and when her lips met mine it was as if I was drunk.

We didn't go to bed together. Not that night. That night, we kissed by the magical fairy light of my Christmas tree. By one in the morning, Lisa walked dizzily out my door and called me the minute she stepped through hers. We talked until three, and fell asleep on our phones.

I didn't want to strip her, and I didn't want to ask. But I wanted to know. I wanted to know not only what lived between her thighs, but whether she liked *sex*, whether she liked *me*. I guess I should have known by then, but there's something about love that makes a person self-conscious and totally neurotic.

When we finally found our way to nudity, we found it in the dark. I never expected it to happen the way it did. We'd just finished tidying the makeshift dressing room when Lisa snapped off the light. Everyone else had gone home by then. We were the last two people in the building. Lisa found me in the darkness and kissed me into submission, tearing into my pants. When she stroked me through my panties, my knees buckled the same way they had the first time I saw her.

I fell at her feet, and she obviously took that as a sign, because she unzipped her pants. The stretchy satin of her panties kissed my cheek. When she'd pushed those down too, I brushed my lips across her pubic hair. It tickled my nose, but I didn't laugh. I didn't even laugh when her erection whacked the underside of my chin.

I bowed to her hardness, finding her wet tip with my bottom lip. She hissed in a way that sounded surprised, and her cock pulsed against my face. When I opened my mouth, she found her way inside, and the darkness subsided. I knew how to do this. I knew she wanted it. We both did.

Lisa was the whole package, with a cherry on top.

Everyone at the theater must have known we were a couple, because the other volunteers stopped talking to me. If I liked Lisa, they didn't like me. That sort of thing. But I was lost in love, and I didn't care what they thought.

During performances, instead of sitting in the house with patrons, I'd sneak into Lisa's booth and watch her work. Her job seemed complicated, but she said she'd been doing it long enough that it felt simple. She worked with a prompt script in front of her—a big binder with the play's script in one column and her cues in another. The lighting and sound boards were huge panels with sliders that she often worked with both hands. I liked watching her fingers move.

The week Sisters in Sin played host to a traveling drag show, I worried Lisa would expel me from the booth. It wasn't "her" show. It wasn't an in-house production they'd rehearsed over the course of a month, where she knew the play inside out. For the traveling drag show, she was handed a playlist of karaoke tracks and lighting effects the performers wanted. I figured she'd have to focus.

That night, I stood at the back of the house instead of

invading Lisa's glass booth. I didn't want to break her concentration. Instead, I inadvertently broke her heart.

At intermission, she came out in a huff. She saw me, but she didn't smile. I followed her toward the stage, but I was supposed to help sell soft drinks in the lobby. It wasn't until the tail end of intermission that I met her at the booth and asked, "What's wrong?"

"I could ask you the same question," she said.

"I don't get it," I said. "Why are you mad at me?"

"*Me?* Mad at *you?*" She cackled.

When Lisa entered the booth, I followed. I had no idea what was going on. "Did I do something wrong?"

She looked at me like she didn't know how to respond. Then she looked at her watch and said, "No time." Falling into her chair, she lowered the houselights and got the mirror ball spinning before turning on the karaoke track and illuminating the duo on stage.

"Do you hate drag queens?" I asked. Maybe that was the issue.

Her expression changed from driven to perplexed. "No. Why?"

"I don't know. Some people do, especially feminists and transwomen, and feminist transwomen."

"Drag queens are fine. I've got nothing against them." Lisa had her eyes on the show, but at least she was speaking to me. "I guess the only thing that bothers me is when the general population confuses people who identify as transgender with drag performers who are just putting on a show."

"That makes sense."

"It's a spectacle, after all. It's a music concert." Lisa glanced back at me. "They're nice guys, these two. But they are *guys.*"

"Oh." I set my hand on her shoulder and felt the tension in

her muscles relax. "I thought maybe that's why you were in a bad mood."

"I was in a bad mood because you've been avoiding me all night."

"What? No!" I couldn't believe she thought that. "I was staying out of your way so you could focus on your work."

She laughed, shaking her head, and her blonde ponytail whipped side to side. "Focus on *this* show? It's easy as pie." She glanced at me and smirked. "Mmm...*pie*."

I wasn't standing far away. The booth was small enough that we could never be farther than an arm's length from each other. But I'd never seen that look on her face during a show. She always concentrated so hard on her work, and I just watched. That night, she was concentrating on me.

Lisa's fingers slipped from the lighting board. She cupped my pussy, out of the blue, and pulled me close. Nobody had ever touched me so forcefully. Until then, even Lisa had only petted me like a kitten. She'd build my arousal up before sinking down between my thighs, tossing me clear over that cliff.

This was different. She slid her hand inside my panties and squeezed my crotch. *Squeezed* it. Her palm pressed hot against my clit while her fingertips dabbed at my cunt.

"Wait a sec," Lisa said, adjusting her sliders. "I need to do a few things here."

She reached up to pause the audio system, then brought up a lighting wash, and she did it all one-handed, without tearing her fingers out of my pants.

"You're crazy," I whispered. The booth was somewhat sound-proof, with audio from the stage coming in through speakers, but I still worried about talking too loudly. What if someone in the audience turned around and spotted Lisa's hand in my pants? Anything was possible.

"Okay, we're good for another three minutes," Lisa said, rubbing her wet fingers over my clit. "How's that?"

"I can't believe we're doing this."

My knees buckled and she raised an eyebrow. "So tell me to stop."

I couldn't. I didn't say a word, only whimpered as she stroked my pussy. She was so self-assured that I wondered if her attitude might be turning me on even more than her powerful fingers rubbing my clit.

Onstage, the queens were singing a song I'd never heard. It was upbeat and playful, and they were dancing with sun umbrellas. But Lisa wasn't looking at them. She was looking at me.

"You're about to fall over," Lisa said. "Don't tell me you're coming already?"

I nodded. I was panting. My heart raced in time with my throbbing clit. It felt huge when she toyed with it—huge and swollen and tender and hot.

"Can you come before this song is over?"

"Yeah," I whimpered, rocking against her hand. It was so tight against my pussy, trapped inside my pants. I couldn't believe I was getting off on her like this. It seemed almost impersonal, like rubbing against a washboard or some other inanimate surface.

"You really think you can come in a minute?" Her teeth gleamed as she grinned.

"Sooner," I squealed, clutching her shoulder for support. She never stopped smiling as I fucked her hand.

"Do it," she whispered. "Come for me."

"I am!" I said, trying not to shriek. The lights in the booth were dim, but if someone in the audience turned around and really looked, they'd see us. They'd see my embarrassing orgasm face while my thighs clenched and my calves seized and my whole body shuddered relentlessly.

"Quiet," Lisa hissed.

"I know!" I *was* being quiet, I thought, but I bit my lip to keep quieter.

"Quiet," Lisa whispered, like a tease, as my knees quaked.

It was too much, too much raw sensation. Her hand slid out of my pants as I tumbled to the rough industrial carpet.

"What are you doing down there, hmm?" Lisa's skin glowed bluish in the booth's weird lighting. "Getting hungry?"

"Yes. Please." It hadn't occurred to me before then, but once she planted that seed I could almost taste her on my tongue. "Are you sure you can concentrate on work if I go down on you?"

"Let's find out," she said, guiding my head between her legs.

The way Lisa's little booth was set up, the lighting board and all that stuff was set on a desk that ran from one wall to the other. And me? I was kneeling underneath that desk, with my chin on her chair, pawing into her pants.

"I can't believe we're doing this." I unzipped her fly, but the rest was tricky. I left it to her. "Aren't you afraid of getting caught?"

"Not afraid enough, I guess." Arching her ass off the chair, Lisa pulled down her pants. Her gaff was the tricky part—it was like a supertight, superstrong pair of panties that she wore over her actual underwear. To keep everything in place.

Her panties came down just in time to catch her next audio cue. "Shit! Almost missed that one."

A queasy feeling came over me. "Maybe we shouldn't do this. I don't want to mess up the show."

"You won't," Lisa assured me. "If anyone messes it up, it'll be me."

"What if someone comes up here to see what's wrong? There's no lock on the door, and even with me hiding under the desk, they'll still know what's going on."

"Not if you keep quiet and stay between my legs," Lisa countered. And maybe she was right. Maybe even with someone spying from the doorway we'd get away with it.

Lisa's naughty parts weren't shy around me. Her cock slid eagerly from the space in her pelvis where she'd tucked it away. Its glistening tip found my lips like we were magnetized. I kissed it sweetly, and she sighed.

"Is that what you want?" I whispered, before kissing all the way up her shaft. Lisa wasn't especially hard yet, but I'd get her there. "Should I just kiss you all night?"

"No, no, no," Lisa moaned, probably a little louder than she'd intended. "Suck it, sweetie."

Her hand slipped off the lighting board and landed heavy on my head. There wasn't much space down there. Good thing I wasn't claustrophobic or afraid of the dark.

As Lisa worked her magic with light and sound, I wrapped my lips around her engorged cockhead. She moaned as her precome spilled across my tongue, salty and sweet.

"I'm not distracting you?" I asked with her tip sitting gently in my mouth.

Under the long desk, Lisa wrapped her big hand around the back of my head. She pulled me in tighter between her spread legs, driving her erection into my throat. I gagged and she released her hold on me, but I didn't draw back. I whimpered, subjecting myself to the sweet pain until my eyes watered.

"Oh, honey," Lisa groaned. "Yes, just like that."

I couldn't see her. I wanted to look up into Lisa's face, see that look of lust in her brilliant blue eyes, her pouting pink lips parting the way they do when she's truly aroused. But the damn desk was in the way. All I could do was imagine the sweet look on her face as I consumed her cock.

"I love it when you go crazy on me." Her voice was keen and hoarse. "Do it, honey. Go crazy."

Lisa always said that stage managers had a presence about them that was both understated and commanding. In that moment, the understated went out the window and all that was left was the commanding. If Lisa wanted crazy, that's what she'd get.

Wrapping my fist around her firm shaft, I sucked the tip as it spilled precome all across my tongue. That sweet juice made me suck harder, faster, jerking her off with one hand while I fucked her with my face.

"Oh god, I can hardly hear the music." Lisa's thighs shook. Her balls pulled up tight to her body, so my thumb whacked them as I stroked her hot and fast.

"Come," I said around her cock. "Come in my mouth, baby."

"My hands are shaking. My fingers..." They landed in my hair, her short fingernails digging into my scalp, making me crazy. "You *are* distracting, honey. I'm going to lose my job. I'm going to lose my mind!"

"Come!" I squealed, working harder to get her there.

"In less than a minute, I've got three lighting cues, back to back to back." Lisa gasped as I hit a sweet spot with my tongue. "Oh honey, I'm shaking all over."

I drew back quickly. "Can't do your job with shaking fingers." God, I wished I could see her beautiful face. "Better come fast, baby."

"You just try and stop me," Lisa grunted, bucking so wildly her chair squealed. Her fingers clenched in my hair and she pulled it hard enough to hurt before she stopped moving altogether. Her cockhead pulsed against my tongue. She whimpered like a puppy as she flooded my mouth with hot cream. It slid down my tongue, and it was gone before I got a good taste.

Another blast rushed my mouth, and I savored this one before I missed it completely. Lisa's come tasted incredible—sweet, tangy, and light as meringue. I loved it.

She started to giggle, "Enough," she said, pushing my head away. "Oh, you're killing me, sweetheart. How am I supposed to work like this?"

"You asked for it," I said with a self-satisfied smirk she couldn't see. I was sitting on my feet under her desk, with my back against the wall. It was dark, and all I could hear now was the music fading away.

I crawled around Lisa's chair to watch as she fiddled with her sliders. The stage went from peachy keen to pool party, all because of her lighting effects. When the performers finished their shtick, Lisa pulled up the volume on the next track. It was a song I recognized, but not well enough to name or sing along. I wasn't really up on popular music.

But the audience definitely was. As the drag queens danced through the intro, the whole audience broke out in applause. When the chorus arrived, everybody sang along. Even Lisa joined in, though she sang quietly enough that only I could hear. I wrapped my arms around her neck and rocked her side to side. Watching our reflections in the dark glass of the booth window, I kissed her hair.

"You're cute," I said, and she rolled her eyes. "What? You are."

Her cheeks burned crimson, but she only stopped singing long enough to say, "Thanks."

TALK NERDY TO ME

Crystal Jordan

I glanced at the clock in the corner of my computer screen: 4:51 p.m. How much longer could I wait and be sure he'd pick up the phone when I called? 4:55 p.m. I watched the minutes tick toward quitting time, my stomach hollow from excitement and uncertainty. 4:56 p.m. I reached for the phone and tapped in the number for IT support. It rang once, twice, and I started to worry that I'd miscalculated.

"IT department. This is Graham."

The rich Scottish burr that filtered through the receiver made my thighs quiver. I'd always had a thing for computer geeks. It's shameful, really, but there it is. Add a sexy accent on top of that, and it was enough to set a girl's panties on fire. It worked for me anyway.

"Hello?" There was a tinge of impatience to the word, letting me know I was about five seconds away from being hung up on.

I cleared my throat. "Hi, Graham. This is Sophie Stevens in marketing."

"Sophie." I could all but hear the smile curving his lips. "More troubles?"

Okay, so maybe this wasn't the first time I'd had technical issues since he was hired two months ago. Then again, I probably wasn't the only female employee who'd had some sudden computer problems that required his personal attention. Unfortunately, I was probably the only one *not* doing it on purpose. Though when I reported those problems was a whole different story. Timing was everything.

"I think I'm beyond trouble at this point. My computer screen went blank on me, then turned blue." At about ten this morning. "I tried restarting twice, but it didn't help. Can you rescue me?"

He chuckled, the sound husky and warm. "How much longer are you going to be in your office? I can stay late for you, if you like."

I liked. More than he could ever guess. "I'm putting in a little overtime today to work on a project, so I'll be in my office. Though, without my computer, there's not a lot I can do." Which would be true, if I didn't have my laptop with me. I tucked it into my briefcase and snapped the lid closed, concealing the evidence. "I really need your help."

"I can come and look the machine over now, but I may have to take it with me to fix it. Have you backed up your files like I showed you?"

"Yes, sir," I drawled, and he laughed.

The scolding about having backups had happened the first time he'd come to my office to fix something. Him standing over me, his face so serious, had made me wet. Every time he'd been back since and said things about hardware and rams and bits and bytes had produced the same reaction. Seriously, was I the only one who saw how borderline pornographic the IT profession was? Not surprising that I took it that way, if I considered that unexplored fetish for techies, but the intensity of it with Graham was stunning. It made me want to do something about all that longing. So, here I was, staying late to see if he might be interested in more than just servicing my computer.

I swallowed, a flush burning my cheeks. "Though I was in the middle of some work when it died on me. If there's a chance to salvage that, I'd really appreciate it."

"I'll see what I can do. Be there in a minute."

With that, he hung up, and I was left to wonder if I was out of my mind. My stomach twisted into a million knots and I pressed my sweaty palms to my desktop, blowing out a slow breath. This was insane. I was at *work*. True, the office had cleared out the moment five had rolled around, but still.

A light tap sounded on my door and then Graham pushed it open. God, he was gorgeous. Thick black curls spilled over his forehead, dark-framed glasses set off brilliant blue eyes, and a square jaw and sharp cheekbones completed the picture. His tall, rangy body contrasted with the geeky image. No doubt why tech support had suddenly become such a popular department with the women in the company. Then again, maybe I wasn't the only one with an unrequited craving for IT guys.

"Hello, Sophie." His lips tipped upward at the corners, the door clicked as it swung shut behind him and his gaze swept down my body slowly. "You look nice today."

The slightly awkward delivery of that compliment did nothing to cool my ardor. It just underscored the fantasies I'd had about him. I fought a shudder as he looked me over, hoping my nipples hadn't beaded, but the way his eyes focused on my chest for just a moment too long told me they probably had. I thought I saw interest reflected in his expression, but I'd thought that before and nothing had ever happened between us. I doubted it ever would, unless I made a move.

Three strides brought him around the desk and I had to tilt my head back to look at him. He was close enough I could smell the light scent of his aftershave, feel the heat of his body. His khaki pants brushed my bare calves, sending a wave of want boiling through me. I had to cross my legs to try and contain the ache between them. The movement only emphasized my need.

He glanced at my monitor and shook his head. "Yes, the blue death screen isn't a good sign." He frowned. "Did you update your anti-malware like I told you?"

Malware. I wasn't even really sure what that meant, probably something to do with viruses, but it sounded sexy coming from his lips. Every time he said something in computer jargon, I all but panted. It was embarrassing, really. "I—I think so."

"Hm. I don't know then." He shook his head. "I prefer Linux to Microsoft, but I think I'm in the minority. Microsoft is too vulnerable to worms. Has it hung on you lately?"

"Hung?" I couldn't help it. My gaze dropped to his fly.

He noticed, and a flush highlighted his sharp cheekbones, but a wicked little grin formed on his face. "Has it stopped working or been running slowly?"

"Sorry, I don't speak computer. It's kind of sexy when other people can." Oh, Jesus. Why had I admitted that? My brain had clearly gone the way of my computer. On the fritz. *That* was my idea of making a move? The floor could open up and swallow me now.

He gaped. "You think so?"

There wasn't a single non-humiliating response I could think of, so I kept my mouth shut. I spread my hands and shrugged, my face as flushed as his.

A truly sinful twinkle filled his blue eyes and he leaned toward me, his voice dropping to a low rumble. "So I shouldn't talk to you about bogon filtering or metasyntactic variables, huh?"

I closed my eyes, fire burning up my cheeks. Embarrassment tangled with desire. This was madness. "Um. My computer hasn't been hanging or whatever. I would have called you. Technology tends to explode around me, so I leave it to the experts."

"Sophie."

When I forced my eyes to open, I found him on his knees in front of me. And wasn't that a lovely little fantasy come to life?

"Yes?"

One dark brow rose. "If you wouldn't mind...I need to fetch your computer out from under your desk."

"Right." I pushed my toe against the floor, scooting my chair back a bit. "Sorry."

"Not a problem, lass." He ducked his head and started unhooking all the cords and cables from the back of the metal box that held the brains of my computer.

Sliding backward, he pulled the thing out and set it aside so it rested against one of the desk drawers. He pivoted on his knees to face me, his gaze suddenly focusing on my crossed legs. I watched his throat work, and his mouth opened as if he wanted to say something, but no words came out. Glancing down, I saw that my skirt had ridden up, exposing an indecent amount of my thighs. I made no attempt to pull the garment down.

"See something you like, Graham?" The question was soft, almost a purr. The look on his face soothed something inside me for having spilled about my little addiction to people fluent in techno-lingo.

He swallowed, his gaze unwavering. I could feel those blue eyes burning into my flesh like a laser. Naked hunger flashed across his expression, and he pushed his glasses up with one long finger. Instead of dropping his hand, he reached out to stroke a fingertip against my knee. He didn't speak, didn't meet my gaze, just focused utterly on what his hand was doing.

The first touch sent a jolt straight to my belly. My sex clenched in helpless want. I could feel myself growing slick as he circled around my knee and feathered his fingers up the top of my thigh. My heart beat a rapid tattoo against my breastbone and my breathing sped. I'd imagined this so many times. Until today, I'd never actually thought it might happen. But this? This was irresistible. A slow seduction.

When his eyes finally met mine, they gleamed with mirth and lust. "VoodooScript, C++, Fortran, Pseudocode."

I bit back a whimper as he edged his finger along the hem of my skirt. I don't know which got to me faster—his touch or his words. "Graham, please."

He dipped down to nudge my legs apart, and I uncrossed them for him. Reaching out, I tugged off his glasses and set them on my desk.

"Well, now I can't see. I'll have to get closer." He didn't sound perturbed about that at all. Leaning forward he brushed a kiss on the inside of my knee and I swallowed. His fingers slipped in to stroke over my panties, and I moaned. My hands gripped the arms of my chair as he traced the lips of my pussy through the lace of my underwear. His lips worked their way up my legs and he bit the inside of one thigh. A sob choked out of me, and moisture gushed from my pussy. I knew he felt it soak my panties, and he gave a little hum of approval that set off sparks within me.

"Lift up," he said.

I arched my hips out of the chair, and he used the opportunity to drag my panties down and off. He stuffed the scrap of lace in his pocket. A groan ripped out of him as his gaze zeroed in on my naked sex. Lava flowed through my veins, a need so hot and sharp I couldn't contain it. More. That was all I could think. *More.* His hands on my knees, he dragged me to the edge of the seat and bent forward to curl his tongue around my clit.

"*Graham.*" His name burst from my lips, the sound caught somewhere between a gasp and a sob.

My fingers slipped into his dark hair, the rough silk of it soft against my palms. I pulled him closer, shuddering as he formed his lips around that tight little bundle of nerves and sucked. My mouth fell open in a silent scream, and I pressed my legs as far apart as my chair would allow.

A jolt of lightning sizzled through me when he bit down on my clit. His palm slid up from my knee, and my heart hammered at the thought of him caressing my bare sex. Then he did, rubbing over the wet flesh until I thought I'd die of pleasure. My head fell back against my chair, my eyes closing at the feel of him teasing my slit. My grip tightened on his hair as excitement shot through me. Oh, god. It felt so damn good. Better than any fantasy I'd ever had.

The breath caught in my lungs when he pierced my pussy with one thick digit. He added two more, stretching me before he began thrusting deep. My sex clenched, and I knew I was seconds from climax.

"Yes, yes, *yes!*" My hips left the chair as I arched hard, my pussy fisting around his fingers.

My eyes snapped open when he hauled me out of the chair and into his arms. Shock reverberated through me when he slammed his mouth down over mine, shoving his tongue between my lips. I could taste my musky wetness mingled with his hot, masculine flavor. It made me moan, made me writhe against him, especially when his palms curved over my ass. I could feel the hard ridge of his erection against my stomach.

God, I wanted him inside me, filling me. Just that quickly,

my recently sated craving crested again, slicing through me like a white-hot blade. My senses whirled as he spun me around, backing me into the desk. He urged me up onto it, and I wrapped my legs around his waist. A groan poured from his mouth and into mine as he ground his cock into my pussy. The rough seam of his fly abraded my clit, the discomfort just twisting with all the other sensations that slammed into me at once, taking me to a place where pleasure and pain merged.

His hands cupped my shoulders, pressing me flat on the hard wooden surface. Plucking at the buttons on my blouse, he worked my shirt open and spread it wide. He traced the edge of my bra, consternation on his face when he reached the front clasp that held it together. Our eyes met and we both grinned. Taking pity on him, I unfastened the clasp, and my bra peeled back to expose my breasts to his gaze. His pupils dilated so that only a slim ring of his blue irises remained, and lust flushed his face.

"You're so beautiful, Sophie." There was a reverence in his voice when he covered my breasts, circling the tips with his fingers. He bent and sucked my nipple into his mouth, batting the tight crest with his tongue.

My back bowed on the desk, a gasp strangling out of me when he bit down on my sensitive flesh. "Please."

A shudder of wicked anticipation gripped me as I heard the harsh rasp of his zipper. Yes. Oh, yes. I squeezed my thighs on his hips as I felt the tip of his cock nudge my opening. Then he pulled away, denying us both. I moaned a protest. His palms pressed to the desk on either side of my torso, his head down as his lungs bellowed for air.

"Graham?"

A growl issued from his throat. "I don't have a condom with me."

Disappointment crashed over me, as did the knowledge that

I'd been so far gone that I'd completely forgotten about protection. That had never happened to me before. Ever. This really was insane, and I still wished it didn't have to stop.

"Well, I don't carry them with me ei—wait, I *do* have some." I sat up and pointed to a small gift bag sitting on one of my filing cabinets. "We had a bachelorette luncheon for Tammy last week and one of the party favors everyone got were fluorescent condoms."

"At this point, I don't care if they glow in the dark, lass." His accent had thickened with need, and I loved the sound of it. He pushed away from the desk and strode over to the bag, rifling through it until he came up with a little foil packet.

On his way back to me, he ripped it open and sheathed himself. He was...bigger than I'd have imagined, his cock a long, hard arc. I wanted to suck him, but I'd barely managed to open my mouth to say so when he shoved his hand in my hair, holding my head still for a rough, demanding kiss. The taste of him burst over my tongue, and I couldn't hold back a moan. It was overwhelming, this dream turned reality. I twined my arms and legs around him, holding tight to this wicked fantasy. The kiss was all lips and teeth and tongues as we battled for control of it, fighting to take and give more at the same time.

His hands moved between us, one palming my breast, and the other gliding lower so he could roll his thumb over my clit. I clutched at his shoulders, whimpering into his mouth and arching my body in offering. My sex clenched on emptiness, needing to be filled.

As if he'd read my mind, the head of his cock slid over my slit, pressing forward one slow inch at a time. The stretch was fucking divine. I bunched my fingers in his shirt, letting my head fall back as I reveled in the feel of him inside of me. Finally. I'd imagined this moment for so long.

His lips moved down my throat, nipping, licking and sucking the tender skin. "SQL, syntax, ANSI, subroutine."

"Shut up and fuck me, Graham!" I huffed out a laugh, but dug my heels into his ass, bucking against him.

He chuckled, his breath rushing over my damp skin, and goose bumps shivered down my limbs. Then he started moving. We both groaned at the exquisite friction. I leaned back on my hands, rocking forward into each of his thrusts. He started slowly, the drag of his flesh in mine an inconceivable ecstasy. Cupping my breasts in his hands, he rubbed his thumbs over my nipples, and my desire boiled out of control so fast it stunned me. Needy little sounds spilled from my throat with every movement he made. He picked up speed and force, his skin slapping against mine. When he rotated his pelvis against my clit, I exploded into orgasm.

"Graham, *Graham*." My inner muscles clamped around his thrusting cock, milking the length of him while he pistoned in and out of my pussy. He rode me hard through my climax, and another one built swiftly on its heels. I cried out as my sex pulsed hard around his, ecstasy dragging me under like a riptide.

One, two, three more thrusts and he buried himself deep within me and groaned, shuddered. He dropped his forehead between my breasts, his breath rushing across my sweat-dampened skin while we slowly came down from the high. Long minutes passed before he spoke. "Jesus, Sophie. That was..."

He shook his head as if he couldn't find the right word. Neither could I. It was indescribable. I let a slow breath ease out of my lungs, a smile quirking my lips. I couldn't believe I'd actually done this. I knew nothing about him, other than that he was a walking wet dream for me. Wild flings weren't my style, but I didn't have a single regret. Living out my fantasy was worth it. I'd do it again in a heartbeat.

Easing back, he slipped out of me. I watched him try to clean himself up as best he could, but I stayed where I was, still too languid to bother moving. He came back to the desk, picked up his glasses, and put them on. There was a clang and he winced. I glanced down and saw that he'd banged his shin into my computer. He sighed. "I'll have to take it with me. I should be able to return it to you tomorrow...but it might take me all day to fix it."

"I can stay late for you, if you like," I said, repeating what he'd said earlier.

"Mmm." His eyes crinkled at the corners, and he brushed his lips over mine, the touch hot and sweet at the same time. "Maybe I can explain what a computational model is to you. Tomorrow?"

Reaching up, I cupped his face between my palms and drew him down for a longer kiss. We were both breathing hard when I let him go. "I'm looking forward to it."

CURRENT
PHOTO,
PLEASE

Devin Phillips

When I joined a stupid "casual dating site," I thought I had no illusions, but maybe I did. For about five seconds, I thought I might meet someone interesting. Pretty soon I knew that wasn't going to happen.

See, "casual dating site" is code for "a supposed dating site that isn't really about dating but looks like porn, so guys join and sensible women keep away unless they're sex workers and then they play games with the guys until they cough up a few hundred bucks and then they fuck them, or they just get the losers to log in to cam sites and pay for the privilege."

And yet, there I was! And I really had only myself to blame.

I don't know what tempted me into setting up a profile at HotBot. The site had nasty ads and far nastier male members, and I don't use that double entendre casually. I'd joined because I wanted to have a few sexual adventures, but I was way too chicken to just post on Craigslist. And I'd been told that if you verified you were a real woman with the staff, they would comp you three months' worth of premium membership.

They did, and it was nasty. Once I had my profile up with an obscure shot of my face and a few of those cropped-down body shots my friend Amanda had done last year or the year before, my inbox was stuffed. I got hundreds of messages all in the span of a couple of days. At first, I sought to respond with a "Thanks, but no thanks," which got me pleaded with, begged at and called nasty names. It only took one day before I stopped responding altogether. After that, I only logged in to bolster my sense of moral superiority and pessimistic disgust with the human race.

Which backfired horribly one night, when I found myself looking at a message from a guy named Clay.

His comments about me were kind and complimentary, but not creepy-complimentary.

His profile said:

> *Looking for whatever feels right. I'm a little kinky, but not hard-core. I've been around the block. But I'm looking for a long-term girl. Meantime, casual is also fine. I'm even down for booty calls if we hit it off. Just be honest. Current photo, please.*

The profile only had a few body shots—which, if the other respondents were any indication, were probably his brother, cousin or some stock photography model. But there was no picture of his dick, which was a big plus, and horribly rare on this site. And Clay apparently liked my profile enough that he'd gone so far as to attach a recent head shot not displayed on his profile.

The second I saw it, my heart jumped. Yum. Oh, yum. Oh, oh, *yum.*

Then that pessimistic disgust I talked about earlier chased my excitement down and beat it to death with a stick.

Come on, I thought. *Don't even respond. What kind of loser thinks he can get away with sending a porn star's head shot? Doesn't he realize if we meet, I'll know he's lying?*

But Clay's message to me was *very* charming. He was black, which I like. Mind you, that didn't mean he was actually black; with online dating, white guys do some crazy shit, as in most other arenas.

But the thing is, his head shot was a picture of a porn star. The chances were almost unthinkably low that it really was him, and I knew that.

And had it been almost any other porn star, I wouldn't have given his message a second thought. But he was named Clay and the guy I was thinking he looked like was named André Clayton.

I had this sense that somewhere, I'd read that the guy's real name was—

It took me next to no time to find it, right there in the Adult Film Database. There he was on his AFD profile: gorgeous and built and magnificently rampant.

Real Name: Clay Emory Higgins.

Didn't prove anything; he was probably still fake.

Any dumb guy could look up André Clayton's real name on the Internet. Just like I did. Right?

Right. I probably would have assumed that was what was going on. Except that I followed a couple of links from the AFD page, and there were these clips, right?

And, well…things might have gotten out of hand.

An hour of André Clayton clips later, I decided this was ridiculous. I decided to go ahead and make my first date from HotBot—an immediate booty call with the two lowest-maintenance men in my little black book: Buzz and Mister Throbby. Our threeway went down thirty seconds later, when I returned from my bedroom with Buzz in my left hand and Throbby in my right, and...well, André Clayton came exactly as I did. Of course, I went out of my way to time it like that.

Exhausted and sweaty, I figured I had to at *least* send him a thank you, right? I knew it almost certainly wasn't André Clayton. But whoever was pretending to be him had given me an effortless orgasm. He might be deceptive, but I'm not in the habit of hit-and-runs. He deserved at least a thanks.

So I wrote the impostor back:

> *Dear "Clay," (ROFL!)*
> *You made my day. André Clayton is the only porn star I would totally fuck with totally no strings attached. Like, right now, any day, any hour. That would be awesome if you were really him. Too bad you're not. But I just watched some clips of his and... wow, it's really too bad. LOL! Good luck, guy. Oh, and you might want to choose a less famous porn star next time. LMFAO!!*

I sent it. That was that, I figured. Right? Right. Right?

Well, I don't know what made me hang out online for another few minutes, "just to see." Sometimes on those stupid "dating" sites, guys sit there and email you back right away...like, in seconds. And always without spell check.

Well, "Clay" sent me back a message a few minutes later, all right. It was spell checked, all right. And it had a brand-new picture.

Dear Devany,
You made MY day, girl. Glad to hear my oeuvre is
still out there and still giving girls as hot as you a few
minutes of pleasure. I hope it was the right kind of
pleasure.
*   I confess I have some dirty thoughts about you*
watching one of my clips and—well, I'll leave that to
my imagination. For the record, here's a new picture.
And that booty call you promised? Any time, Dev.
Any day, any time, day or night. I live in Cooper
City, so...
*   And for the record...I don't think I'm that famous.*
I work in a bank now. But then again you've heard of
me, so maybe I'm wrong.

André Clayton (LOL!)

Ulp. There was his picture. A couple of years older, perhaps,
but...shoulders. Holy shit, those were really his shoulders. (Well,
only one of them was in the picture, but...it looked authentic,
right there about three inches under his head.)

The guy had these eyes that were seriously not to be
looked into unless you wanted to find your panties in his
pocket and your legs around his waist. All of his movies spent
time from the woman's perspective, looking up into those
eyes. Totally different than most porn—I think whoever he
worked with must have understood that he had plenty of
female fans.

And speaking of female fans, *those lips.* I think that I'm not
alone in saying how important the lips are. His were...yum.
Twenty minutes earlier, I'd been thinking about those lips doing
something I'd never let any guy do.

And there they were twisted in a cocky grin, inches from a computer screen displaying my message.

I downloaded the picture. I opened it and blew it up. Was this a Photoshop job? If it was, it was a good one. How do those weird forensic guys figure out if something is a Photoshop job? I realized it probably wasn't. That was really my message, right there on his screen, and the time stamp in his photo was current.

And there was *still* no picture of his cock. Major plus.

I started to realize he might be real. I almost fainted. I definitely hyperventilated a little. I'd had first aid training by then, though, so I guess it was okay. I'm not kidding when I say I actually had to lie down on the floor, wearing nothing but my underwear and a T-shirt, until I'd calmed down a little.

When I finally recovered, it was *way* past my bedtime. I had to be at work in the morning. Cooper City was about an hour away, and no, I wasn't going there. I wouldn't meet this guy till I knew for a fact that it really was him, and then—

Any day? Any hour?

Please. As if. I doubted it was really him. Somehow, in like the five minutes it took him to answer my message, some weird white asshole living in his mom's basement had Photoshopped a picture of André Clayton's head in front of a picture of a screen with my message on it.

That seemed much more likely than that I'd just promised my favorite porn star no-strings-attached sex. Right?

Right.

Dear "André Clayton,"
Okay, I don't know if you are just really committed
to this or what but you could always put your money

where your mouth is. If you are still up, why not send
me a cam invitation? LOL, I probably won't get one,
but thanks anyway. It was still fun playing the game.
And yeah, if you were really André Clayton...um,
yeah. I'd be up for that.

I sent it before I could freak the fuck out and remove that last
part. The second I sent it, I wanted to slap myself.

And, yeah, he was still up, I guess. I got a cam invitation
just a few minutes later. I get them all the time, and I'd never
accepted one, but I had certainly heard about them. I expected
it to be some guy with his junk in the camera. But I had to
satisfy my curiosity.

Well, André Clayton's junk wasn't in the camera, but I'd already
seen plenty of it that evening. And if anyone was guilty of flashing
her junk to the camera, it was yours truly. I'd been so spinny with
excitement I hadn't even bothered to put on my pants.

It was him, all right. I was embarrassed. He was a gentleman
about it. He barely even teased me about thinking he was a fake.
He told me I was even hotter than my pictures. He told me he
loved the name Devin so much better than Devany, which was
my stupid slightly fake online name. And he talked to me for a
full two hours, the time passing effortlessly until we were ready
to sign off, and he told me with a charming grin:

"I'm gonna hold you to that promise, Devin."

I turned red. I giggled and tittered and tossed my hair and
flirted.

I said, "How can you? You don't even have my phone number."

"So, then...give it to me."

"Yeah," I said. "As if!"

"Please? If you give me your number, you're off the hook."
He grinned. "But my offer stands."

It took two more compliments about my hair and a promise that he wasn't a serial killer, and I did a very bad thing. I gave him my number.

I'm as easy as pie sometimes.

Clay didn't tease me anymore about the "promise." He never even brought it up, and when I did, it wasn't my promise, but his.

It was just three days later that I came to my senses and told him, "Mind if I come to Cooper City?"

His voice rich with pleasure, he asked, "Why would you come to Cooper City, Devin?"

"Why do you think?" I laughed. Then, in a soft, deep, quiet, serious voice, I said: "To fuck your brains out."

"In that case, I don't mind at all."

I told him I wanted his address well in advance, so I could email like five friends with it just in case he turned out to be some kind of freak.

He said, "Look, Devin, I'll do you one better. I'll tweet it."

I gulped. "You've got a Twitter account?"

"Yeah, I still have a few fans hanging around. I'll tell 'em whatever you want." He laughingly added, "That way, if you disappear, the cops will know just where to look."

That was good enough for me. I didn't make him tweet, and I only emailed his address to my mom. As far as she knew, I was going to Cooper City to look at a car for sale.

Because mine was sort of on the old side...but it still made the drive to Cooper City in forty minutes flat.

We met up in a café not far from his place, because I'd always heard you should never meet a guy at his place. Doing so means you commit. I was about as committed as a girl can be. I'd gone there wearing makeup, which is a pretty big deal for me. I also wore a skirt, which is almost unheard of. I thought I looked pretty good, and Clay's expression told me that he thought so, too. We'd already spoken for several hours on the phone and cam at that point, and the whole reason I'd driven to Cooper City was to make good on my promise of a booty call.

The crazy son of a bitch wore a tie to a booty call; is that crazy or what?

As soon as I sat down I started to blush, because I was talking to Clay, but André's eyes were right there in front of me, practically undressing me. Or maybe it was just because I'd seen them in so many point-of-view videos, undressing whoever was on the other other end of his cock at the time. It was a little too familiar for comfort, and his resonant voice didn't make it any easier. When André said, "How was your drive?" all I could hear was the word "drive." Which was enough to get me flustered all over again.

I had been there for maybe five minutes when I decided this was silly. We both knew why I was there.

So I said, "If we were to go back to your place right now... could I leave my car here for a while?"

"No problem," he said. He glanced at the counter. "They know me."

I felt a stab of minor jealousy.

"Because you've done this with other girls?"

Clay stared at me with a strange combination of amusement and sadness.

"Because I come here every morning and write poetry in a notebook for a couple of hours."

I said, "Oh."

He told the guy at the counter what kind of car his "friend" had, could they make sure not to tow it? No problem.

I'd been there less than ten minutes when I found myself in his car.

Then I was glad he wore a tie. It gave me something to grab when I pulled him onto me.

He leaned over and kissed me hard. I let go of his tie and put my arms around him. His hand found my thigh. I wasn't used to wearing a skirt. It felt intensely erotic to feel his big hand on me. Vivid images of what it had done made me tremble all over. Then Clay took the lead. He didn't make me wait. His hand slid gently up my thigh while his big dark eyes looked deep into mine. I just kept looking back, letting my thighs rest just far enough apart that he knew I wanted him to continue.

He did. When he found I wasn't wearing underwear, I bit my lip and laughed, embarrassed.

"I'm sorry, it's stupid," I said. "I just kind of thought...I've never had a booty call before. I thought I should—"

"No explanation necessary," said Clay. "I think it's hot. I've always liked a woman who knows what she wants. You be as big a slut as you want to be, or don't be one at all. Either way, nothing could make you less sexy."

Blushing fiercely, I quipped: "You've never eaten my cooking."

He frowned disapprovingly and gentled me with a kiss. Under my skirt, his fingers found what they needed. I was warm and wet and crazy for him, already deep into my third day of thinking of him constantly. Two of his fingers went in easy, and I clutched his arm. I shuddered. I whimpered.

He kissed my neck. I trembled all over.

"I better get you home," he breathed in my ear. "Before you explode."

"I may explode anyway," I said.

"That's good, too," he said. "I'll put you back together."

He made me wait for long, tortured minutes as he gently explored me, his fingers caressing my sex. His thumb teased my clit. The son of a bitch knew what he was doing. I smelled him. I tasted his mouth: Earl Grey and spit. As his lips made waves on that perfect spot between my jawline and neck, my eyes crossed.

"Did you really mean what you said?"

"About what?"

"I can be as big a slut as I want?"

"Sure," he said.

I flattened my palm on his chest and pushed him back into the driver's seat. I leaned over the gearshift and planted my mouth on the front of his jeans. I went for his belt.

"Whoa," he laughed. "Don't get too crazy. They know me here."

"You're the one who put your hand up my skirt," I said playfully. "And you said I could be as big a slut as I—"

I never finished the sentence, and I didn't say anything more for a while, because my mouth was very, very busy...right there in the parking lot.

His cock was a gorgeous piece of heaven. It tasted good and clean and a little bit musky and I could smell him as I lowered my lips to the midpoint of his shaft. They say they do things in porn that make guys look bigger, but I don't know about that. All I know is that André Clayton's cock was just exactly the way I remembered it from a thousand fantasies. It tasted and smelled and felt like I'd spent many nights with it, and I guess I had.

He lasted, too. I was lost down there for what must have been ten or maybe even twenty minutes, while he kept lookout. We were parked at the end of the parking lot, so I guess we had some privacy. He never told me to slow down, and he never stopped whispering things to me. Soft, dirty things about how good that felt, but never a caution that I needed to stop or he'd come.

He knew how to last.

When I'd had my fill, for now, I came up quick and swiveled his rearview to take a look at myself. My makeup was ruined, my hair mussed.

"I shouldn't have looked," I said, embarrassed.

"Devin, remember who you're talking to. I've seen girls at their worst."

"Yeah," I scoffed. "With professional hair and makeup!"

He tucked his cock away. He zipped and buckled. "With just-fucked hair and runny eyes." He ruffled my unruly mop and caressed my wet cheek with his thumb. "And you don't have either yet. It's a long night," he said with a grin.

"Promises, promises," I said, sniffling.

He put the car in gear.

I didn't put my seat belt on.

His place was a cozy little two-bedroom apartment in an anonymous-looking apartment complex. He had wine in the fridge, but I didn't need it. What I needed was him on the couch, and my mouth back down where it belonged.

This time, he didn't just let me work. Instead, he reached down and smoothly opened my blouse. He leaned over and unzipped my skirt. He worked it down over my hips nice and easy, and teased his foot between my knees so he could push my skirt down my legs and over my shoes. He undid my bra. I was naked before I even knew it, and Clay slid his hand in my hair to guide me off his cock.

"Greedy little slut," he said. "Some of us haven't even eaten yet."

He led me to the bedroom and playfully pushed me on the bed. I watched as he stripped down, feeling that eerie familiarity with a body I knew like the back of my hand but had never seen naked before. He was gorgeous. He'd put maybe twenty pounds solid on his ebony frame since the porn I had watched, seemingly every ounce of it in his shoulders and arms. Don't get me wrong, I'm not some kind of muscle girl. But...on some guys it just looks so *good*.

He was even hotter than when he'd "worked." I wanted to ask him how the hell *that* worked, but he didn't give me much time to look. As soon as he was naked, he was on me.

His wet mouth kissed its way down my body. He pressed it to my pussy, and those perfect lips did...*things*. But it was the tongue that really blew my mind.

When it comes to porn stars, they're known for different things. André Clayton was known for this. And he did it in a way that made my heart pound...same way he seemed to do everything.

But in movies, eating pussy is a spectator sport, I guess. I've watched a lot of those movies, and I think you have to kind of lean back, lick without licking. He couldn't get *into* it...not the way he could in private. With nobody watching, the visuals didn't matter.

Except that I was watching, and the sight of André Clayton down between my legs was *crazy hot*.

He licked *hard*. He knew how to suck just a little as his tongue worked. He knew how to use his hands—I don't mean inside me, at first, but *all over me*. On my thighs. On my belly. My breasts, my hips and my side. And then he took my hands and pulled me bodily onto him. By the time he pulled one hand away and slid two big fingers inside me, he had me right where he wanted me...there in the palm of his hand.

I'd never had an orgasm from being licked before. I certainly didn't expect it. So when I realized it was going to happen, I wanted to warn him. But why?

Clay knew what he was doing.

He made me come easily, as if it was no effort at all. He seemed so in control that it made me feel that much smaller and helpless. What the fuck did I think I was I doing? Having sex with a porn star?

Yeah, I guess that was what I was doing. Part of me still didn't believe it as the trembling sensations went through me again and again. I put my hands down on his shoulders and pushed, very gently.

"I want you," I said.

When he looked at me, smiled and went back to eating me, I started blushing.

He took his time teasing me, making me wait for another five minutes of exquisite licking. At first I was almost too sensitive to tolerate any more of his tongue. Then somehow, Clay brought me back down to earth.

He knew just when to stop and lick back up my body and kiss me. I tasted pussy. He had a condom from somewhere, opened and ready. He put it on quickly with one hand.

Then he was in me, and I held him close. He started to move like a dancer, slowly, caressing me inside. It didn't feel like fucking...it was more like a massage.

Wrapped around Clay's big, muscled body, I starred in my own private André Clayton production. It was a director's cut... twenty minutes longer than usual. It didn't have a money shot. He was up deep inside me when he came, and I listened to his cries with a soft wave of ecstasy going through me.

This isn't real, I thought. *I'm jacking off, right? I'm, like, home with my vibrator?*

Nope. When my mom called three hours later to ask if I'd bought the car, she didn't get an answer and thought I was dead. Thank god the cops won't take a missing person report for a full twenty-four hours.

Oh, Mom was pissed.

But I was...*busy.*

As far as my mom goes, to this day Clay Higgins is the guy who was going to sell me his car, but liked me and asked me out instead.

"What an interesting way to meet someone," she sometimes says.

"Um," I say. "Yeah. What are the chances?"

And as far as the rest? Well, it didn't take long for Clay Higgins to match André Clayton's history for delivering reliable orgasms.

Not like I kept an exact count for either, but in maybe two weeks, it wasn't even a contest. And that's only because it's a long drive.

He still makes me weak when I hear him say, "Drive." And the distance from my computer to André Clayton's bed is now about thirty feet...from the office to the bedroom of that cute little cozy two-bedroom in Cooper City. What an interesting way to meet someone, huh?

Yeah, I guess. What are the chances?

BODY WORK

Cora Zane

I t's nothing to worry about, Katy, she just needs a little body work."

That's the thing about Joel Sutton I like the most. Aside from the fact he's gorgeous and I've known him most of my life, he's the hot-rod revving, busted-knuckles kind of mechanic who can appreciate the special bond between a girl and her car—in this case, a Laguna Gray, 1970 Corvette Stingray.

I stood with him in the open bay facing Winchester Road, trying to catch a breeze to save me from the blistering August heat. An industrial fan rattled away in the open brightness of a doorway at the other end of the garage, and above the rhythmic clatter of the fan blades, the tinny sound of a radio playing Zydeco music echoed from a speaker at the back corner of the business.

Joel squatted down next to my car, the scuffed toes of his combat boots crunching over the grit on the bay floor. A week before, some jerk driver hit my front fender while I was parked downtown. As if that wasn't bad enough, on Tuesday, my car—my *baby*—started making a horrific grinding noise whenever the front wheel turned.

While Joel examined the bashed fender, I took the opportunity to admire his broad shoulders and the tribal designs curling around his powerful forearms. I've always had a thing for gearheads. More specifically, dirty, tattooed, garage boys.

With his spiky black hair, inked sleeves and ice-blue eyes, Joel definitely fit the bill. Beneath that navy work shirt with the oval name patch on the pocket, he's tan and ripped. I've come across him working shirtless at least once every summer, and what a body. Completely lickable. For that reason, I've never missed an oil change. There's something rewarding about watching an incredibly sexy mechanic servicing you, even if it's only the car getting the lube job.

He stood up and walked around to the driver's side, stopping by the front wheel well. I had no idea what he was doing since the car hadn't taken a hit on that side. Before I could ask what he was looking for, he leaned forward, rested his cheek on the glossy, gray hood, and smoothed a raw-boned hand across the car's flared fender.

I froze with my pen an inch away from the insurance check I was supposed to be signing. The sweeping movement Joel made was slow and deliberate, a caress of flesh over fine machinery. His scarred knuckles contrasted sharply against the spotless, shiny paint. I easily pictured him exploring the curve of a woman's hip in much the same way.

I couldn't tear my gaze away. Joel's face was both serious and serene. He had to be looking for...something. I wasn't sure what. Lines and angles, dents and dips. Things only a mechanic would know to look for.

Whatever the case, he brushed his hand across the fender

again, and I imagined him stroking his hands over my body with the same careful attention. A tingling sensation started at the base of my spine and quickly spread liquid fire through my belly. My brain launched itself on a mental pleasure trip that featured biting, lots of heavy breathing and raking my nails down Joel's bare back.

A sharp pulse of pleasure made me squeeze my thighs together. I'd grown damp in two seconds flat. Then I realized Joel was no longer focused on the car. Instead, his gaze had fixed on me.

Somehow, I'd managed to snag his undivided attention. Our gazes locked. He stood straight and regarded me in a way that made my nipples harden beneath my slouchy T-shirt. For as long as I'd known him, he'd never looked at me like that before.

"I'd love to know what put that look on your face."

Heat was slowly creeping up my neck. I pretended I didn't know what he was talking about and lowered my eyes to the clipboard in my hands. I scrawled my name on the back of the insurance check, intensely aware of Joel watching me. I dotted the i's and crossed the t's on the repair agreement then placed the clipboard on the ledger stand tucked against the wall between the two open bay doors.

He went on with his causal inspection. "We've known each other a long time. Why is it we've never gotten together?"

The question rang in my ears. My face had grown rosy hot. I was both flattered and intimidated by his sudden interest. "I guess it never occurred to either of us to give it a shot."

A tiny white lie. How could it hurt?

It's a little embarrassing when I think about how often he's played a role in my fantasies. In fact, one of my favorite daydreams involves me riding him cowgirl style in the driver's seat of my car—in this very garage. Take that well-worn fantasy and add my vibrator to the equation, and I swear I can come in five minutes flat.

He stopped directly in front of me. "Are you seeing anyone?"

"Not currently." My heart was galloping a mile a minute. "What about you?"

He picked up one of my long ginger curls and coiled it around his finger. "I'm still looking."

"For trouble?" I folded my arms across my chest.

"For someone special," he corrected me. Amusement lit his eyes. "But I guess trouble will do. Do you think I've found it?"

I licked my lips. "I guess that depends on why you're asking."

He caught the side of my face and blindsided me with a tender kiss that quickly turned hot and heavy. I slid my hands beneath his shirt to feel him skin to skin, and his hand found its way beneath my T-shirt to squeeze my breast. Every stroke of his tongue notched up the heat.

Soon Joel's hand snaked past the waistband of my cutoffs. By then my heart was thundering in my ears. I widened my stance, allowing him better access, and he didn't disappoint me. Rough fingers delved beneath the lacy edges of my panties and massaged my clit in tight circular motions. I gasped against the side of his neck and held on for the ride.

Joel kissed my hair. Then my temple. His breath tickled my ear.

"Tell me. How do you like to get off?"

Heat flooded my body. No one had ever asked me that before. I wasn't quite sure what to say or how to react, but my panties grew damp as I thought about dragging Joel to the floor for a quick, messy fuck. I pictured myself rough-riding him on the concrete floor of the bay. Then on the ugly, plaid couch in the back office. And, of course, the front seat of my car was always a welcome option.

"I like to cowgirl." I cringed at how breathy and unsure I sounded, but it was impossible to think straight with his fingers strumming my clit. I added quickly, "And sixty-nine."

"Those are *positions*, sweetheart. I want to know what turns you on. What makes you want to come just thinking about it?"

I ground myself against his fingers. "What you're doing is working pretty well."

He stopped rubbing me at once, and I had to bite my lip to keep from whimpering. His expression chastised me. "That's too easy, Katelyn. Try again."

"I don't know what you expect me to say." It was the truth. I'd drawn a total blank. My mind worked furiously to come up with an answer he'd approve of. I mean, of course I know what I like—what turns me on. I like lots of things, lots of positions. Buzzy toys. Oral sex. How could I get more specific than that?

"I...I like to know I'm pleasing someone." If nothing else, it was true.

Joel nodded. "I like that, too." He had started rubbing my clit again. "What else do you like?"

Was this conversation really happening? The whole situation seemed surreal. The garage. Joel with his hand down the front of my jean shorts.

I was a hair's breadth away from reaching orgasm, and it annoyed me that I couldn't properly reciprocate. The front of his jeans boasted an obvious bulge, so I reached for it and began massaging his dick through his clothes. When he thrust himself hard against my hand, I nuzzled his stubbled cheek then traced the tip of my tongue over his lower lip. "I like *you*."

Another truth.

"I like you too, Katy." A slow smile curved his wicked mouth.

He delved a finger into my cunt, and I sighed with pleasure. "You know, it's strange. I've always pictured you being the type to try topping from the bottom—don't ask me why."

I frowned. I had no idea what he meant. I started to ask him, then I shook myself and pulled back enough to look up at him. "You've always pictured me?" Had I heard him right? Had he just admitted to fantasizing about *me*?

I searched his face for clues, but his expression had turned inward, contemplative. I wondered what was going through his mind. The intensity of his gaze had me tingling from my scalp to the soles of my feet. He continued to pump his fingers in and out, and I could feel a sweet rush building. He kissed me again, and at the same time, his free hand worked its way back under my shirt. He rubbed his fingertips across my nipples, and I bit my lip to keep from sighing.

"You like that?" he asked quietly.

"Absolutely."

"And if I asked you to fuck me?"

A knot of pure lust shivered through me. Did he think I'd say no? Hell, I was ready to fuck him *right now*, preferably until we were sweating, screaming and raw. I angled my hips, taking his fingers deeper. "I'd be a good girl, of course. I'd even let you pick the position."

"Is that right?"

My brows went up. He really had no idea. Joel represented my gearhead fantasy come to life. I've always found him deliciously attractive—him, and workingmen like him. Provider types. Men who work with their hands and aren't afraid to get dirty and sweaty. Bonus kudos if they're concerned about giving a woman pleasure.

Joel hit every one of my hot buttons, and if I had to guess, I'd bet there weren't very many women who had ever said no to him. Big surprise. I wasn't about to say no to him, either.

The sound of tires crunching over gravel drew my attention toward the road. Joel's fingers went still, and he swore under his breath as a rusty red pickup truck pulled into the drive and parked next to my rental car. "It's Ed Finch. Nice old guy, but he's a talker."

Joel nipped my earlobe and withdrew his hand from my panties. I let out a frustrated whimper. His expression was sympathetic as he took a step back and pulled his shirt down to help hide his erection. "Maybe we can pick this up again later. Think you can come back around seven-thirty?" He watched me reach down my shorts to rearrange my panties and raked his teeth across his lower lip. "I'll make it good for you. I promise."

"I hope you're a man of your word," I ground out. I was so turned on and tuned up I wondered how I'd drive home.

"Always." Joel's eyes skimmed over me with such blatant desire it made me giddy.

Okay, fine. If he was up for a challenge, so was I. I agreed to meet with him later, and that was that. Joel wiped the hand that had just explored my pussy on a shop rag and started across the bay to greet the old man who was just now climbing out of the beat-up truck.

Let's just say I've never been a fan of daylong anticipation. I was practically shivering with excitement by the time I reached Joel's garage that night. I'd been in a crazy-horny state when I'd left his shop earlier that day, and since then I hadn't been able to focus on anything but my approaching date with him. Now that I was here, it was a relief just to know he was close.

Joel waited for me in an open bay door. I turned off the headlights and climbed out of the rental car I'd been driving since I'd turned over my car for repairs. I locked up with the wireless key fob then headed in his direction, stopping briefly to give him a quick kiss before I ducked under the door.

While he closed us inside, I looked around as if surveying an alien landscape. I'd never been in the garage after-hours before. It was quiet and the air was surprisingly cool. My Stingray was parked in the same spot where I'd seen it earlier.

A single strip of overhead lights glowed throughout the shop. Without the old fan clattering near the back door, the air carried the faint tang of gasoline, grease and motor oil. Anticipation prickled my skin, and I was glad I'd worn an easy-access pinup dress to meet with Joel tonight.

The dress had no crazy buttons, no hard-to-reach zippers and I'd worn my clear plastic stripper shoes with it. Easy on, easy off. At any moment, I could simply kick off my shoes and pull my clothes off.

I turned around to see Joel doing just that. He was pulling his black T-shirt off over his head. Now that we were inside where there was better lighting, I noticed he had showered and changed into fresh clothes. He tossed his shirt onto the ledger stand and faced me. I hadn't seen him shirtless since last summer when he'd been mowing the grass outside the shop. His pierced nipples instantly drew my attention. When had he gotten that done? I debated asking him, even as my fingers itched to play with those sexy silver rings. I let out a shaky breath.

"Good to see you too," he said as he came closer. "You look amazing."

"So do you." It was the truth.

When he was within reach, I caressed my thumb over one of his nipple rings, tracing the tiny O. He shivered.

"They're sensitive," he told me. I continued my exploration, following my fingertips with a flick of my tongue. He inhaled sharply then captured my hands and turned me around so my back was against his chest. "I've been thinking about you nonstop since this morning."

He slid my dress up my hips, leaving it bunched about my waist. A warm hand caressed my bottom. "No panties. I like the way you think."

"Yeah, well, I aim to please." Smiling to myself, I rubbed my bare bottom against his crotch and felt the evidence of his arousal.

He buried his face against my neck and inhaled my scent. "Mm. Why don't you take off this dress?"

No games, no pretense. I could appreciate that.

I caught my dress by the hem and pulled it off over my head. He waited until I'd tossed it onto a tool chest with an open bin of what looked like bottled oils and sex toys before he reached for me again.

His hands were work roughened, but his touch was gentle as he caressed and squeezed my breasts together and captured one of my nipples in his mouth. He flicked the tight nub with his tongue, and a shower of sparks rained through me.

I sighed with pleasure, and he went down on his knees behind me. Leaning forward, I braced myself against one of the raw I-beam supports that ran from floor to ceiling and widened my stance. Starting with my asshole, he darted his tongue against me, then licked a path along my slit. Finally, he reached my aching clit and tickled it with his tongue. I shivered and melted against him.

"Wait a second." Joel stood up and steered me toward a mechanic's rolling board on the floor nearby. "There." He dragged the board closer with a foot. "Kneel down on the creeper."

I slipped off the clear stripper sandals I'd worn just for him and carefully knelt down on the board, clutching the sides for balance.

Holding on for dear life, I allowed him to pose me ass up, head turned to the side and resting on the "creeper." He knelt behind me then and parted my pussy lips. Cool air struck my most vulnerable places. I was incredibly wet.

He worked a finger into my cunt and another into my asshole. Despite how slick I was, his fingers were large and calloused and it took me a moment to adjust to the double penetration. When he combined sucking my clit with finger-fucking me, I worried I wouldn't last.

Whatever his plan, my gentleman gearhead didn't try to rush me. He flicked and sucked my clit with perfect patience and precision skill. He never let up, not even when he had me teetering on the edge and every delicate touch had me squirming.

Heat scorched my face when I thought how I was probably drenching his tongue, but if it bothered him, he didn't say a word about it. I was grateful for that. With or without a round of messy oral sex, after a full day of waiting, I desperately needed to come.

And then I did just that.

I climaxed in a hard, sudden rush. Flashes of light pulsed behind my closed eyelids, and I heard the roar of my blood pulsing in my ears. Through it all, Joel crooned praises and continued to finger-fuck both my slick holes. I shuddered and shook. He stayed with me until my body stopped quaking, and I'd collapsed onto the creeper board in a panting, boneless heap.

"Damn, you're beautiful." His voice was deep, raspy and ripe with lust.

After the orgasm he'd just given me, I definitely wanted to return the favor. Judging by the bulge in his jeans, getting me off had obviously done its part to turn him on. Still jittery from peaking, I sat up and began unbuckling his belt. I had it all mapped out in my head. He'd just earned the blow job of the century, and I wouldn't rest until I'd tasted his come.

I'd just unbuttoned the top button on his jeans when he laid a hand over mine to stop me.

I looked up at him. "Everything okay?"

"Everything's perfect." He took my hand and pulled me to my feet. "Come with me. I have something else in mind for my turn."

We didn't go very far, only a few feet away. He let go of my hand when we reached my car, and at first, I had no idea what was going on. Then I saw the red tool chest behind him and remembered the bin of sex toys I'd noticed earlier.

I waited while he fished through the box. He seemed to know what he was looking for. When he pulled out various bottles of lube and a strap-on with a large black dong attached to it, a frisson of worry danced down my spine. I knew he intended it for me, but I'd never—I mean, I didn't want him to think I was inexperienced, or simply being a smart-ass, but I had to ask. "What's all this?"

"It's how I like to get off," he said as he unzipped his jeans. "I like to be penetrated. Preferably by a hot willing woman."

And if I asked you to fuck me?

His eyes devoured me as he sat down on the edge of a tool chest and began to strip off his boots. "I also like to keep things discreet—in the garage, I guess you could say. Of course, I get it if you don't think you can handle fucking me. Just say so now if that's the case."

My mouth went dry. He was so straightforward and nonchalant about it. Was he challenging me or offering me a chance to leave?

I'd always suspected Joel was the type of man with whom you had to scratch the surface to see what's beneath, but I never would have guessed he had a kinky side. I didn't know what to say, but I was flattered that he trusted me enough to ask me to fulfill his needs.

"So I take it we're still game on?" he asked.

"Of course." Like I'd really skip an opportunity to have him any way I could get him.

Mischief glittered in his pale eyes as he stood up and shucked his jeans. His cock was thick and rock hard. Everything I'd hoped for.

"Have you ever pegged a man before?"

My speechlessness must've revealed what he already knew. He laughed softly.

"Well, I consider it an honor to be your first." He tossed his jeans into a plastic chair. "Come here and I'll help you buckle up."

I was glad he offered since I'd never worn a strap-on before and wasn't exactly sure what leather strap went where. I watched his deft fingers work the straps free of the buckles. I ran a finger along the length of the dong. "Whose strap-on is this, anyway?"

"It's mine."

I blushed at his firm tone, but I was relieved to know it didn't belong to someone else—an ex-girlfriend, maybe.

It took a few minutes, but once he had me buckled in, he stood back and admired his handiwork. I now stood before him in nothing but sheer, thigh-high tights and his strap-on. I took the massive licorice black dong in hand as if it were a natural cock and posed for him.

"Damn that's hot." He leaned down to nibble my tiny nipples, first one then the other.

My breathing quickened. I wrapped one hand around his hard cock and cupped his balls with the other. He had such an incredible body, all hard muscle, tattooed abs and pierced nipples. Remembering his piercings, I leaned forward and flicked one of his silver rings with my tongue. A hiss of air rushed from his lips.

We chose a clear jelly from the bin and lubed my artificial cock together, our hands making slick noises over the black flexi vinyl. The dong seemed slightly thicker than average, and was probably a good nine inches long. The shape was like a real cock, veined, with a well-defined mushroom tip. He guided my hand over it as if it was his mission to teach me how to jerk off.

"Fuck." He blew out a breath. "I love watching you do that."

One glance at his raging-hard cock and I knew he meant it. Weak-limbed and shaky, I held out my hands for more jelly.

The amount of lube we used made his skin glisten. His eyes blazed down at me as I squeezed a final dollop of lube into my hands and slicked it between his parted thighs. I'd already glossed his balls and his cock. This time I massaged jelly against the rim of his asshole before breaching him with my fingers.

Joel spread his legs apart. I penetrated him with first one finger, then two, and I didn't stop until I was able to finger him the way he had my cunt earlier that day. It wasn't long before his breathing grew harsh and his eyes slipped closed. I pressed my thumb firmly against his taint while working my fingers inside him, and he wavered a little on his feet.

I tugged at a pierced nipple with my teeth, and Joel's asshole clenched around my fingers. He tangled his hand in my hair, jerking my head back. Firm lips crashed down on mine, and as he kissed me, the spicy flavor of my pussy on his lips made me think of leather, cinnamon and unspoken secrets. Kissing him brought back memories of every dirty fantasy I'd ever had.

His calloused hands kneaded the cheeks of my ass. Glancing down between us, he brushed his jutting cock back and forth against the strap-on dong. "I want you to fuck me hard, Katy. No holding back. Can you do that?"

Before I could answer him, he turned away and braced his hands on the hood of my car. I waited for him to get comfortable, then I stepped up behind him and prodded his glistening anus with the tapered head of my artificial cock. It slid into him quickly, easily, though for a moment he tensed up. He didn't seem to be in any pain, so I gripped his hips and started fucking him.

It was awkward at first, the motion of pumping into him. My rhythm was off. I braced my hands on his hips to steady myself. Even then we moved out of sync, and I had no choice but to go slow.

"Fuck me harder, Katy. That can't be all you've got." His displeasure stung my pride.

Heat flooded my face. I froze. Almost chickened out. But I didn't want to fail him—not Joel, the object of my filthiest daydreams. Besides, I'd sort of made a promise.

Instead of pulling out, I slapped him hard across the ass and slammed into him, balls deep. Joel went down on his elbows so fast, for a moment I thought I'd hurt him.

When I saw he was okay, that he'd started to prop himself up, I pushed him down by the nape of the neck and pinned him against the hood. "Did I tell you to lift your head?"

He went instantly still, and after I drove into him hard and deep a few more times, he shifted his weight forward and tipped his pelvis, the action lifting his ass higher to give me better access. I whispered how hot I thought he looked, and built a rhythm that had him pressing back against me. Gradually my thrusts became more even, more regular.

"Fuck yes. Like that," he murmured through gritted teeth. "Deeper. Ah, fuck yes."

I raked my nails down his broad back. "You love that big dick in your ass, don't you?" When he didn't answer me straightaway, I gave him a hard hand across the ass and pulled out of him.

A hiss of displeasure left his lips. He answered me then. "Yes. Yes, I do!" His hands clenched into fists against my car, and a strained noise left his lips. "Please, Katy, don't stop!"

I slapped the dong against his bottom for good measure, and smiled to myself when he spread his cheeks for me. I squeezed into him again, and he gave a soft cry of pleasure.

This time when I penetrated him I gripped the tops of his thighs and held on. His strong muscular legs flexed slightly every time I pumped into him. To show my approval, I leaned forward and licked his back. Then I bit him. Joel made a soft sobbing sound and rested his head against his arm.

I'd been fucking him for probably ten minutes when suddenly his muscles tensed and he groaned. His stomach muscles contracted beneath my splayed fingers. His cock bobbed slightly. He was close to coming, so I held him in place and fucked him harder, without mercy. Well, he said he wanted it hard. I intended to give it to him just the way he wanted it.

I leaned over him so my breasts rubbed against his sweat-damp back while I thrust into him. The new position allowed me to reach around Joel and cup his balls. I massaged his sensitive skin, and he tipped his head back in ecstasy.

"Do you want to come now, Joel?" I asked near his ear.

He choked on a sharp breath, and his nostrils flared. A muscle ticked in his jaw. No man had ever looked sexier. Clearly he was hanging on by a thread. When he finally spoke, his voice was thick. "It feels so good." He hung his head and pushed back against me. "Please, fuck me. Make me come."

I wrapped a hand around his cock and began to jerk him off. His muscles tensed again, and his legs trembled. His asshole tightened around the dong. Joel braced himself against the car and made a move to take over jerking off, but I slapped his hand away. Resigned to let me take control, he bowed his head in submission.

I jacked his cock from base to tip in slow, firm strokes, taking my time with him, just as he had taken his time with me. I kept a steady rhythm, timing the flow of the hand job with the thrusts of my fake cock. His breathing quickened, and soon I had him squirming beneath me—exactly how I wanted him.

I continued to pound into him until finally Joel shuddered with release. A garbled string of unintelligible words came from his mouth as the first hot spurt of his come shot between my fingers.

He thrust forward through the tunnel of my hand, still coming, erupting, spilling milky drops across the hood of my car. He uttered my name on a harsh breath. It was a heady experience. Completely sexy—and secretly, a recurring fantasy of mine.

Only when he'd been reduced to a quivering mess of aftershocks did I slip out of his body. By then, my legs were tense, the muscles burning. Breath heaving, Joel collapsed against my car. Mindful of the come spot he'd just made, he rolled over onto his back and looked at me. "That was incredible."

He was sheened with sweat and looked exhausted. Totally fucked down. Inwardly, I beamed with pride.

He was so sensitive from his orgasm he could barely stand it when I kissed my way down his body and sucked his softening cock into my mouth. His muscles jerked, and he tolerated my buff job for less than a minute before he grabbed a fistful of my long hair to make me stop. I bit my lip to hide my glee. Not a bad night's work for shy little Katy.

Joel made a subtle, chiding sound and pulled me against him for a kiss. Our tongues dueled, both flavored with each other.

At last, I pulled away and stroked my hand across his washboard stomach, taking a moment to appreciate the view. I considered taking off the strap-on and tossing it back onto the tool chest, but I was somewhat used to wearing it at that point. Instead, I carefully crawled up Joel's body and straddled him. I pretended not to notice how slick my inner thighs were. I was pretty sure he didn't care about that, anyway.

The way he looked at me made my skin tingle. I sensed him puzzling me over. Honestly, I'm not sure why. Maybe I'd surprised him. I'd definitely surprised myself.

Amused, he watched me rubbing the fake cock idly against his bare stomach. "Having fun with that?"

I dipped the head of the dong into his navel. "Absolutely."

He folded his arms behind his head and sighed. A thoughtful look crossed his face.

"I'll probably have your car ready by next Friday," he said. "Maybe after you pick it up we can go over to my place. What do you say? Dinner and drinks?"

Excitement blossomed low in my belly and quickly spread through me. "Sounds like fun."

I reached out to toy with the silver ring piercing his left nipple. We'd been so caught up in each other when I'd first arrived I hadn't gotten the chance to play with his piercings as much as I would've liked. Oh well, it looked like I'd be getting another chance soon enough.

Joel stroked his thumb along my lower lip, and the intimacy

of his sensual touch lit me up inside. I felt radiant and glowing, and even though I was satisfied for the moment, I was already looking forward to next Friday. I could hardly wait to take his hot body for another joyride.

UNDER HER AUSPICES

Jeremy Edwards

There were no figures in Vibeke's museum. Every canvas, whether Impressionist, Postimpressionist or Fauvist, was a landscape or a still life. Even the abstract paintings were always abstract *things*, never abstract people (though I had to read every plaque to make sure of this).

And so when I entered the building each day at quarter to six, after the tourists had all gone, it was, as the romantics say, like I was the only man in the world—and Vibeke the only woman.

I would have spent this daily interval—between leaving my office and catching my train—at the little art museum next door, no matter what type of person presided over it. It just so happened that the presiding official was a type of woman I would otherwise have wished for excuses to be near. She was a portrait of meticulous competence, tasteful sophistication and refined intellect, with an eager mirth in her eyes and a look of fresh-scrubbed vitality to her flesh, as seen in the two scoop-like servings revealed where her blouse gave the word. But under the circumstances, no excuses were necessary. I was here legitimately. I was "the public" she welcomed.

"I keep my cityscapes in the northern gallery," I heard her say on the phone one day, her testimony bouncing proudly out of the small skylit office she inhabited. "*My*" cityscapes. At other times, it might be "my" floral gallery, or "my" eastern corridor that I heard her reference. The sense of loving possession was like a caress to my balls: I wanted Vibeke to take possession of *me* somehow, too. The art belonged to the public, of course, as it should, but still I appreciated the element of benign, symbolic ownership that Vibeke's curatorial love had earned her. It was as if I could taste the kiss of her cunt down the banister-like edges of each golden picture frame. In my mind's eye, Vibeke's pussy gilded as it glided, her juices an alchemist's wet dream.

Her voice, whether tickling my ears from the office or heating my cheeks when she spoke to me directly, was, like Vibeke in toto, a confection of aesthetic passion coated in elegant professionalism. Her Northern European accent made me think of tiny, beautiful pastries coupled with afternoon coffee, of unself-conscious nudity in townhouse hotels.

Next time I was within earshot while she was on the phone, she was speaking in Norwegian—but doing a dance I nonetheless recognized, which could be summarized as follows: *I really ought to get going now...but I don't want to be abrupt...and I'd honestly rather keep chatting with you than return to whatever's on my desk...so I'll sort of circle around signing off, while letting this friendly conversation extend itself.* This subtext was conveyed to me through rhythm and tone of voice only, as Vibeke wound down—yet didn't—her call with a buddy or sibling or European art-world comrade.

Finally, after saying one last thing in her native tongue,

she added, "Because it is Friday," in her contraction-light English—following that word *Friday* with a brief, happy laugh that sounded to me like white wine and weekend sex, before saying "Okay, bye," and hanging up.

Though there were actually other people in the vicinity—I'd arrived closer to five-thirty that day—I doubted anyone would have registered what had transpired. So in the weeks to come, I would view my textured memory of Vibeke's Friday laugh as a kind of private treasure in my personal museum.

We were alone as usual, however, on the day she nearly knocked me over—literally, physically almost bowled me over. I had a habit of cornering too tightly and too quickly from room to room, while Vibeke's museum had a thermostat whose adjustment required ducking out of sight around one of the aforementioned corners. With the adjustment made, the curator sprang efficiently into the doorway, just as the patron sailed blithely into her path. Unlike in the classic "meet cute" collision, Vibeke and I (a) had already met, and (b) were both conscientiously looking where we were going. It was simply that we were going there too fast. And as we headed toward this unplanned bodily intimacy we were in fact looking, with helpless surprise, right at each other's faces—which felt intimate in itself, in the instant I had to process it.

My reflex was to stick my hands up and block her from slamming into me. With Vibeke standing a couple of inches taller, this had the unintentional effect of sending my palms straight for her breasts, which luxuriated within her neckline as if lounging in a hammock. But Vibeke's reflexes were as sharp as my own, and her hands braced my elbows in time to keep that particular contact from being made. Her gaze met mine with concern—it had frightened her to think she'd nearly run me down—and her solicitousness felt like worry, not for a stranger, but for a friend. I was, her eyes told me, a familiar presence in her realm, perhaps even a presence she valued.

I smiled. Her eyes relaxed and then drifted down to the small gap between her chest and my fingers, where the action had frozen. She released my elbows, looked at my face again, and laughed. The tension dissipated in a grab bag of "sorrys," relieved giggles and "are you okays?". I had an erection.

"I am very careful of my paintings," she quipped, "but I should be more careful toward my visitors."

"*My*" visitors. At last, she had claimed me.

The incident also offered us the seed of that precious commodity, the in-joke. An in-joke that, if nurtured properly, could ripen into that even more precious commodity, the *running* joke—a ritual that would grant the laughter Vibeke and I conjointly enjoyed a unique, relationship-specific flavor.

And so, on my next visit, I said, "Be sure to ring a warning bell before you adjust the thermostat, now." And a week after that, when I'd been away for a few days on business, she acknowledged my return with, "Welcome back, Mr. Thermostat." I relished the mutational whimsy whereby I had *become* the thermostat...and yet, I noted, there was sense in the nonsense—because Vibeke did indeed dial my temperature upward.

One day, by the mere good fortune of reversing my normal route through the galleries, I had the privilege of watching her hang a painting. She straightened the new acquisition, then stepped back and sighed, evidently moved anew by its beauty, her professional crispness melting as the miniature emotional orgasm of art appreciation overcame her for an instant.

I wondered if it had made her panties wet; then I wondered what kind of panties we were talking about, above the charcoal-pencil stockings that shaded up into the vanishing point beneath her ass-aware black skirt.

She caught me looking at her while she looked at the canvas. "Such a perfect little seascape," she commented, graciously indicating I was welcome to share this moment.

"Yes," I agreed heartily. "You know, I'm a software developer these days…but I actually did a master's in art, and my thesis touched on these sorts of Italian Riviera scenes."

"Oh, that is terrific. Perhaps you would like to do a presentation sometime? Here, under my auspices?"

Needless to say, under her auspices was precisely where I wanted to do a presentation.

And what lovely auspices she had. I was certain of this, though the skirt showed me only the general outlines, and left it to my mind to envision the detailed contours. This, naturally, was an assignment my mind was quite content to tackle, again and again: depicting Vibeke's auspices, and what it would be like to frolic under them.

"You should email me if you would like to schedule your talk," she continued. Then she laughed. "In the afternoon, please. I am always greeted by great sheaves of European email when I arrive in the morning." Apparently, to this expert in objects of two dimensions that miraculously evoke three, even electronic communications had a palpability, and I adored that. Meanwhile, I swallowed an internal "ooh la la" at the absurdly titillating overtones I invested in the words "European email."

"I suppose that's the disadvantage of being on the sleepy side of the Atlantic," I said. She chuckled liberally at my turn of phrase. The laughter breathed out of her mouth like courtesy overwhelmed with delight.

"You come here every day," she said. It was not expressed

as a challenge or a puzzle; it was simply an observation.

"I try to." I explained about the five-thirty quitting time and the six-twenty train.

"Before today, I did not know you were a scholar of art. But of course I knew you were a lover of art. After all, one does not come to the galleries for sweets or for kisses."

Though the clipboard in her hands suggested she was in midtask, she made no move toward resuming whatever task it was. She lingered there with me in her southern gallery, her lips holding the pose that the unexpected word *kisses* had left them with.

I stared at her as I heard my voice tremble out. "Where, then, does one go for...the kisses?"

Vibeke blinked, smiling more warmly now. "Even in a museum, there is the office. Yes?"

Yes. What better place to flourish under Vibeke's auspices than in Vibeke's office?

As she ushered me in, her right nipple making deals with my left shoulder blade, I observed that her sanctum included a couch, out of sight from the foyer. The room smelled like hot chocolate.

She closed the door and turned me toward her, with firm slender fingers on my shoulders. The promised kisses came down from her lips to mine, and I thought how wonderful it was that she stood taller.

I placed my hands on her bottom and pulled her in closer.

My squeezes found response, not only in her body but in her conversation. She had a way with a rhetorical question, I learned: "It could be said that the bottom, in a sense, is everything, could it not?"

I squeezed hers harder. "And yet you display none of them in your museum," I whispered playfully.

"So true. But I will display this one, for you. Then you, I suspect, will reciprocate. I think it will suffice?"

In a moment she was posed before the sofa with her back turned. She unzipped her skirt, and I saw black bikini panties zoom down with the outer garment, an underwear passenger on an express elevator.

Her ass, now bared, exceeded my high expectations. Rounder, nobler, and unimaginably harmonious with her hips, Vibeke's bottom seemed at once classically callipygian and utterly distinctive: no buttock globes, I was sure, had curved along exactly those trajectories, ever before. No specialist, whether art historian or calculus professor, could possibly demonstrate otherwise.

Yes, to use her idiom, it "sufficed," all right. Sufficed to suffuse me with—well, I'll call it happiness. I more or less threw myself at her feet, clasping her calves, kissing the indentations behind her knees, and gazing up at the landscape of her derriere. How could something so precise in form be sculpted from such softness? I freed my cock from my trousers.

I studied Vibeke's ass even more closely. Symmetry being overrated, she sported a singularly fetching dimple along the southern border of her left buttock. If you can imagine Vibeke's bottom as a smoothed out—very smoothed out—and idealized—*very* idealized—map of Ohio, the dimple would be in the neighborhood of Cincinnati.

Still on my knees, I straightened my torso so I could reach and lick the undersides of her cheeks. Her pussy was fragrant—beautifully fragrant in my face now, as she parted her thighs and asserted the jut of her derriere, pressing its convexity against my mouth.

As Vibeke responded to the buttock love, I couldn't tell if her repeated staccato syllable was an English "yeah" or a

Norwegian "ja." Either one worked for me. But when I stood up and began to explore her slippery cunt entrance with my finger, she shifted to a soft, pan-linguistic cooing. Her thighs shifted, too, as she centered her nerves around the nucleus of sensation we were crafting for her.

I moved my right hand toward her clit while I fucked her with my left. But Vibeke grabbed my fingers and guided them back to her right cheek, using my digits to grope her own bottom flesh. Then she licked her finger and proceeded to take care of her clitty, while I tickled her cunt and fondled and slapped her behind. We wallowed in the bliss of this steady state for as long as she could stand the pleasure...and then Vibeke clenched, squealed, came, stammered, squirted and shrieked.

She clutched my angled cock while soliciting my feelings about the next installment. "May I enjoy your ass before we fuck? I mean, you will wait for the shagging while I pleasure your buns?"

I nodded, and she fished her panties out of her skirt and handed them over. "Here, you wrap your dick in these while I touch you. The silk for your cock, and the leather for your thighs." She directed me onto the leather couch.

I'd never before had my buttocks celebrated. But there I was, facedown with my cock besilked and my trousers and shorts furled halfway down my legs, and Vibeke—sweet, warm, bare-bottomed Vibeke—seated on my upper thighs and massaging my ass with a passion.

I'd long been conscious of—or shall we say *obsessed* by—the bottom as a highly erogenous zone for many women, a theme that Vibeke had so pleasingly illustrated. But damned if I'd ever realized how erogenously sensitive *my* ass was. The sustained attention of a woman's hands over my buns—all over them—was exquisite. At least it was exquisite here, in the context of

Vibeke's obvious enthusiasm for the spare, firm terrain of my butt. With every pinch, pat and caress, my ultra-aroused cock twitched into the cool silk on the leather cushion, and my thigh muscles answered the curator's fervor by tensing libidinously against the roundnesses of her own glorious derriere.

Soon I became aware that my ass was now getting a *one*-handed massage—and that Vibeke was *ja*- or *yeah*-ing her way to another orgasm, her fingers playing her clit and pussy so energetically that the hairs on my ass could sense the motion. I held back from coming, but, oh my, Vibeke did not; I felt her whole body shaking atop me. Afterward, she kissed a dozen places on my buttcheeks—feverishly, lovingly. I'd never known anything like it.

She grinned with satisfaction when she rolled me over, and licked her lips at my readiness. She eased herself onto me with a slow grace, and I articulated my ecstasy in a raw, lustful sob.

Then she went wild: bouncing on my shaft, nudging her mound against me on the downstrokes, working me thoroughly and vigorously...ravening on me without inhibition, and with a clear intention of making me spurt quickly and uncontrol-lably—which I did. She frigged herself on me as I lost myself in the release, and through my orgasmic haze I watched her eyes climax.

Vibeke said she'd use her en suite bathroom to clean up, while I stumbled out to the public men's room. Yet when I returned, I found her seated on the office floor—her back against the couch, her knees spread wide, her long fingers in her juicy hole. She looked up when she saw me, and I fumbled for speech.

"Oh. Didn't you—did I—should we—?"

"No, it is all good," she affirmed. "I always take an extra one afterward." She blushed. "A private one."

I nodded my blessing—not that she required it. And with landscapes and still lifes at my back, I blew an *au revoir* kiss to the only woman in the world.

"Yes, I will see you here tomorrow, Mr. Thermostat," said Vibeke. Her fingers waved at me from between her open thighs.

ICE-CREAM BOY AND SPRINKLE GIRL

Kathryn O'Halloran

Every night at this time I hear the music, at first barely audible over the noise of the cicadas, then growing louder and louder until it stops just outside my house. Calling me to it. Weakening my resolve.

He stops here every night, even though it is the last house on the street. After this, it's only parkland and nothing, the very edge of the city. He stops, even though there are no children on this street and the only potential customer is me. He sits there, playing his music, trying to lure me out.

The first few times I was easily tempted. I didn't know then. But he'd look down on me, his floppy fringe falling in his face, and ask me what flavor I wanted. I'd look up at him in his tight T-shirt, and I'd think *You, you are the flavor I want*.

He is Asian. I think Korean. His face is slightly feminine but his body taut and strong. Not hard in the way that most white boys I've dated are hard but sleek and slim despite the muscles. He wears a smudge of eyeliner and his long hair tied back in a ponytail, and he has the longest eyelashes I've ever seen. He looks like a prince. An Asian prince.

I wonder if this is a vacation job for him while he studies literature or music or something faintly exotic. Maybe he's a hipster, driving an ice-cream van in a totally ironic way. Or it's his parents' ice-cream van and he's forced to help out over the summer. I think about him a lot.

I think about how those arms would feel if I ran my fingers along them. I think about the softness of his shiny hair. I think mostly about his bottom lip, so lush and full of possibilities. I wonder what he looks like from the waist down because I never get to see that part of him.

But, in reality, I do nothing. I take my ice cream and pay him in coins and run back inside like a scared little wimp cursing myself for not making a move. Until I stop going out altogether rather than deal with my failure. I sit inside typing fantasies about him while he idles outside. My fingers hit the keys but my mind goes other places until he gives up and drives away. Then I delete everything I've written because it makes no sense.

The fading sound of his tinny music taunts me as he leaves.

But not tonight. It's the end of summer and soon he won't come to my street. Already the days have reached that peak of heat where they feel like they are going to burst open.

Even though I've just showered, I'm already sweaty again. Summer is like that around here. The humidity so thick you feel like you can drink it in. I've dressed for the occasion in a singlet top that is so very low cut. When I stand at the window of his van, he'll have no choice but to look down into my cleavage and then, I imagine, it will all go smoothly from there.

I wait for him to come closer, the music calling me through the night and the cicadas going crazy. Some cars and the distant notes of a television. And him.

At last, I hear the van stop. I wait, just in case tonight, for once, someone else decides to come out, but I am impatient too. I don't want him to drive off before I work up the courage to go out. I watch from behind the curtains until I can't stand it any longer.

When I open the front door, I hesitate for a second, but the mosquitoes swarm fiercely around the front light ready to attack. A breeze stirs up scents of jasmine and magnolia and honeysuckle. The sky glows purple and red. And in front of me I see the bluish light from the van.

I watch him as I cross the lawn, framed in the window of the van. He's in the shadows so I can't see the expression on his face. Has he been waiting for me to come out? Is that why he drives down here every night?

Around him, painted peaks of soft serve rise up from the candy pink, looking vaguely dirty as though some kind of sexual connotations could be applied to them. I'm not sure what. Even if you put air quotes around "soft serve" and add a cheeky wink, it's not going to get anyone hot.

He has changed his hair. It's slightly shorter and a lighter color. It bounces in waves around his face. I wonder if he's had a perm. He's also wearing more eyeliner than usual. These are things I have been raised to believe are effeminate and unappealing in a man. I look at him and they are as appealing as all fuck.

At the side of the window, the menu lists an array of ice-cream options. I pretend I am deciding even though I always have the same thing. I adjust the elastic in my hair, screwing up my face with indecision. What does my choice say about me? Boring? Childish? Dumb?

I ask for a standard vanilla cone.

"Sprinkles?" he asks.

I pause. Do I? I want sprinkles. I want sprinkles of his man-love. I want sprinkles of his hands all over me. I want sprinkles of... I nod my head.

He hands me the ice cream and I wrap my lips around the soft-top curl. I scoop it and flatten the top then twirl my tongue along the sculpted curves. I flick the rainbow-colored sprinkles off and look up at him through my lashes, hoping he is enthralled, then slowly work my tongue from the bottom of the soft-serve mountain to the very top in one smooth movement.

"You have sprinkles on your nose," he says.

And my dreams dissolve. I realize I can never be a temptress. I'm no vixen, no femme fatale. I'm a woman with sprinkles on my nose.

But he reaches out with a napkin to wipe it off. He can't take his eyes off me. I lean in toward the window but it's a little awkward.

"Come around," he says, and he nods to the door at the back of the van.

I bite my lip. I'm going in the ice-cream van. He opens the door to the candy-colored fantasy world within.

I am inside the ice-cream van, and he is so close to me in this tiny space. He wipes the sprinkles from my nose, and then we stand slightly apart. Not looking at each other. Not knowing what to say.

"Ah, so this is the ice-cream machine," I say, because saying anything, no matter how banal and lame is better than standing around in silence. I absently play with the handle.

"Be careful," he says, "it's a bit trigger-happy." He sweeps a lock of hair from his face, tucking it behind his ear. As he moves, the van rocks slightly.

He is really fucking close to me now, so close he brushes against me. Almost close enough for me to feel the beating of his heart. What do I do? Should I leave? Should I stay? Should I throw my arms around him and shamelessly begin?

He inspects me with a scrunched-up face. Then he puts his finger in the sprinkles container and wipes some on my nose. He steps back, sucking on his sprinkle finger, and leans his head to the side in appraisal.

"Sprinkles suit you."

His smile is goofy, and I can't help but smile back. Then he leans over and licks the sprinkles off my nose.

He is slightly shorter than me but that is not a problem when we kiss. I stroke his hair, and it feels so soft. His kiss is gentle and sweet and that bottom lip is like a life raft to stop me drowning. I press harder against him, but he doesn't respond. He continues with his sweet, gentle kisses as though he has his own pace, which won't be hurried.

"Do you like that, Sprinkle Girl?" he whispers.

"Sprinkle Girl?"

"My name for you is Sprinkle Girl."

I laugh. "Okay, Ice-Cream Boy." I laugh some more. Sprinkle Girl and Ice-Cream Boy: we sound like a cartoon crime-fighting duo.

"Is that funny, Sprinkle Girl?" he asks, then bites on my earlobe.

I press against his body, which is as hard and lean as I imagined, and nuzzle into his lime- and coconut-scented hair. He bites harder, enough to make me yelp in pain.

"You taste good, Sprinkle Girl," he says, and his voice is breathy and hoarse.

He sucks on his finger again and then dips it in the sprinkles. I hope that he isn't intending on using those leftover sprinkles on some kid's ice cream tomorrow. Then he paints a line of sprinkles down my chest and I stop thinking as he licks them off.

When he kisses me again, it's firm and rough, not gentle like before. I am pressed up against the counter. I wrap my fingers in his hair. He's got an air of sweetness like the sugary ice cream has permeated his skin, and his mouth tastes of rainbow sprinkles.

He lifts me up onto the counter. I'd have thought I'd be too heavy for him to lift, he is such a scant boy, but he lifts me as though I weigh nothing at all and I realize those aren't just air muscles.

When he removes my shoes and rubs my feet, I lean back against the window, reveling in the bliss, but the glass rattles behind me and I shoot forward. Ice-Cream Boy grasps my ankle and tickles his fingers along the arch until I wonder how I ever enjoyed being with anybody else.

His hands move up my legs, stroking and circling and tickling. I balance wonkily on the edge of the counter but the feeling of his hands on my knees and his mouth against my skin makes me tingle with the anticipation of what is to come. He reaches up under my skirt, his head resting between my knees, and soon his hands work their way around to my inner thighs.

"You are so soft here, Sprinkle Girl," he tells me, and he reaches over for more sprinkles.

As he presses the sprinkles on my legs, he says, "I knew you'd be here tonight."

"Why's that?"

"It's been two weeks. Two weeks is the longest anyone can resist me." He grins up at me then begins licking the sprinkles from my thighs.

Ice-Cream Boy is more arrogant than I'd imagined—I laugh but I can't deny his claim.

As his tongue moves higher up my legs, I sigh and relax, and the glass rattles again. Bam, like it's going to fall right out of the frame. I jolt forward, reaching for something to stabilize myself, something close and solid.

What my hand has clenched around is the handle of the machine and, before I realize it, I've knocked that lever down. The soft serve oozes out, squishes through my hands and splats around the van—big globs of white cream—on the roof, on the wall, on the front of his T-shirt.

We both giggle loudly then fall silent. He shakes his head to flick the drops of ice cream from it and we stare at each other, then he grabs my hand and sucks the ice cream from my fingers. The way he licks is like a cat, tongue darting in and out of his mouth.

He peels off my top and rubs ice cream over my breasts. The cold sensation against my hot skin is magical—my skin is goose-bumped from the cold and from desire—but soon the ice cream melts in sticky rivulets that run down my belly. He laps them up, moving quickly up to my breasts. He covers my sticky ice-cream breasts in sprinkles, and I wait for him to lick the confectionary off.

Instead he reaches for his phone.

"What are you doing?"

"Taking a photo." He winks.

The hell he is. Next I thing I know that will be on Twitter and going viral. I'm not having the world looking at my ice-cream-sprinkled boobs.

He snaps.

"Give me that. Delete that photo now!"

I jump off the bench and try to snatch the phone out of his hand. He laughs and raises his hand above his head so I can't reach it. As I jump, the van wobbles. I squeal, and while he is distracted, I poke him in the stomach so that he drops the phone. I grab it and look at the photo. It's not bad and you can't see my face. He can keep it.

Before I can say anything though, he pushes me against the wall of the van, holding my wrists. He takes the phone back then finally gets around to sucking my rainbow-candy nipples. And he is strong. Too strong for me to resist.

He licks my breasts clean while I arch my body toward him. I want him sucking harder, rougher, but his touch is teasing. I start to realize that Ice-Cream Boy, for all his prettiness and charm, is not to be taken lightly.

"So sweet," he murmurs as his lips move from left to right. "Luscious."

He bites on my nipple, hard and sharp nips, and I grab him by the waist, my thumb probing the curve where his hip bone rises from his jeans. It's not just the ice cream that is sticky and wet but all of me, especially when he pulls down my panties and works his long, ice-cream-cold fingers between my legs. And all the while, he watches my face with a cheeky grin.

"Are you melting, Sprinkle Girl?" he teases.

How do I respond? Yes, I'm melting. I want to bite him, to sink my teeth into his neck. I want to lick and suck and taste him but he holds me back. It is him working me, and all I can do is thrash and moan. I am indeed melting.

The lights of the van flicker on and off; I want to close my eyes but he won't let me, tells me to open them, to watch him, to watch his face. So I watch his face, I watch every bit of lust and arrogance flicker across it.

When he stops, I whimper. He strips off his T-shirt and peels off his jeans so that he stands before me with just a medallion on a chain around his neck and chunky rings on his fingers. He juts out his left hip and displays himself for my admiration. I have never had a man display himself like that for me before. Everything about him is long and lean except his thick, hard cock. Everything about him pleases me.

Soon he has me back up on the counter with my legs spread wide and the stainless steel edge cutting into my thighs. I wonder if this is hygienic. After all, it's a food preparation area. But I don't think too much or protest because I want him inside me.

He slides his cock into me and it fits just right, as though out of all the cocks in the world, this one has been custom-made just for me.

He brings his face close to mine now and stands, not moving. It is such exquisite agony. I hold my breath and my fingers grip tight to the edge of the bench. I don't want to be the first to move.

But I can't control my twitching hips and I can't control the moans and I can't control my need to touch him.

I reach out and stroke his face, the skin soft and smooth. That's enough of a sign for him. He pounds me hard and each thrust makes the van rock and the cones and cups and plastic straws from the upper shelves rain down on us, tumbling onto the floor. I laugh because it's so crazy and dazzling and he's so very pretty even with his face twisted up while fucking me.

"Mmm...you feel nice, Sprinkle Girl."

I lean back against the window with its rattles that grow in intensity, but I am safe with Ice-Cream Boy. He reaches for handfuls of soft serve to spread across my body, smearing the cold, creamy mess on my skin. He rubs and licks and squeezes my nipples while fucking me but, with each thrust, he looks into my eyes as though challenging me to believe that anyone could be this good.

The air is alive with sugar and sex and pleasure.

As I come, I twist my fingers in his hair and scream "Ice-Cream Boy, Ice-Cream Boy!" I slide on the counter but his fingers hold me tight and he stays with me until I can stand it no longer and I scream for him to stop.

When finally he pulls his cock from inside me, globs of white cream spray up just like the soft serve earlier, hitting the walls and hitting my belly where they mix with the ice-cream mess. His grin now is lopsided but with little trace of shame. I am covered in melted, semen-flavored soft serve and it just seems so completely funny that all we can do is laugh.

When I come to my senses, I want to shower and clean this mess off me. My singlet is buried under a pile of paper cups; the skirt hangs from the freezer. Ice-Cream Boy opens a cupboard and hands me a roll of paper towels but that just makes it worse.

Before I can run inside to clean myself up, he grabs my wrist.

"Where are you going, Sprinkle Girl?" he asks. He bites my earlobe again. "I'm not finished with you yet."

I see the sign on the back of the van door: OFTEN LICKED, NEVER BEATEN.

Nodding at it, we giggle again.

So I slide into the passenger seat beside him, and we drive away with the music playing. Ice-Cream Boy and Sprinkle Girl, hungry for more adventures.

CLOSE SHAVE

Alison Tyler

There was no reason on earth for me to enter the barbershop. I'm a girl, after all, and this place was clearly for men only. Not that there was a sign stating the rules—one of those internationally understood outlines adorning bathroom doors. But the attitude was drenched in testosterone. In the window, a cactus grew obscenely out of a ceramic pair of pants—a prickly penis, if you will. Old *Playboys* died faded deaths on the sundrenched table. Shiny retro barber chairs stood in a row like good little soldiers.

But none of that mattered.

I only wanted him.

Whenever I closed my eyes, there he was. A relic, like those chairs. Good looking in an old-fashioned way that suited the place. He had black, slicked-back hair. Sailor Jerry tattoos on his forearms. A razor strop hanging from his station. He did men's cuts and shaves. With a fluffy brush and warm towels. Like in the old days—old days long before he was born.

I had no reason to enter the barbershop, but I stepped inside when I knew he'd be by himself. I'd walked by the shop often enough to have memorized the hours he worked.

He glanced around helpfully. Obviously, I'd come into the wrong place. I couldn't be looking for my boyfriend or husband because there was nobody else there. I couldn't be looking for a cut, because I was a woman. That's what his eyes told me in the split second of silence between us. But I took a deep breath and sat in his chair.

"Ma'am—" he started.

"Oh no. Don't 'ma'am' me," I said quickly. "I'm not married."

"Miss—" he tried next.

I shook my head. "Miss" was too young. Too girly. And here I was, about to ask for a shave.

"We're not one of those...those *unisex* salons." There. He'd done his job. He'd warned me off. He waited for me to climb out of his chair, apologize for my error, be on my way.

"I don't want unisex," I said, "but I *do* want sex."

He met my eyes in the mirror. I didn't look away.

"I'm here by myself," he said.

"I don't want to fuck the two old guys," I told him, explaining what I thought was obvious. "I want to fuck you."

He had to laugh. "Those old guys are my dad and my uncle."

"Then it's a good thing they're not here," I said. "Or maybe I'd get you in trouble." I eyed the strop. He saw where I was looking.

"*I* wouldn't be the one to get in trouble," he said. "You're talking like a girl who needs to be taken out behind the wood-shed."

Those words let me know I'd chosen correctly. This was the

right man. He would give me what I needed. But then he looked at the clock on the wall above the mirrors and said, "You have to go."

I didn't budge. I had saved up all my self-confidence for this moment. I was not leaving without the correct change.

He licked his lip. He was wavering. I could feel his will begin to shake.

"I've seen you," he said.

I nodded. "Twice a day. When I walk that way to work." I pointed. "And that way home."

"You always glance inside."

"Always," I agreed.

"Come back later. Tonight. Nine o'clock."

I slid out of the chair. Then I leaned up on my tiptoes and kissed him. There was that cactus erection in the window, men's magazines featuring girls who had gotten their implants long before I'd lost my training wheels, and then there were the two of us. He kissed me back, almost in spite of himself, and said, "You have to go."

"I'll see you at nine. For my shave."

I winked at him before hurrying from the shop.

I'd been planning this tryst for months. I'd learned everything I could about Tommy. I knew he wasn't seeing anyone. My coworker Chelsea was friendly with his sister. She had told me about the women he dated. Those goody-two-shoes types who fit the cookie-cutter mold of what ladies' magazines tell us of how women are supposed to behave. That wasn't me. I'd never be one of them. I'd given up trying a long time ago.

But I knew I was his type. His real type. All I wanted was for him to spread shaving cream all over my pussy and zip away the fur with a razor. I wanted to feel the warm towels after. And then—oh yes—I wanted to feel his tongue.

Chelsea had told me he only dated girls his family approved of. Chelsea insisted I would never get that nod of approval. I didn't care about any of that. I only wanted him.

When I returned at nine, the store was closed. The sign said so, hanging off-kilter in the door. But I didn't believe the sign. I saw a light on in the back, and I opened the door, the bell overhead jangling to announce my entrance. Tommy walked in from the rear, and he didn't seem surprised to see me, but he did seem pleased.

"What did you mean about the shave?"

On the table was a bottle of wine and two glasses. I hadn't noticed that before. He lowered the shades and I poured myself some red. The *Playboys* were gone, too. He'd cleaned up the place for me.

"I mean," I said, "a shave." I sat on the leather couch in front of the coffee table, and I spread my legs.

"This isn't happening," he said.

I hiked up my skirt. "You do shaves," I said. "I need a shave."

"You need to put some panties on is what you need to do. This isn't how girls are supposed to behave."

"I'm not the kind of girl who behaves," I said.

He seemed torn for a minute. And I was thrilled when he walked to my side and dragged his thumb roughly between my pussy lips. Swollen. Juicy. He licked his thumb and looked at me, and then he said, "This isn't how things work."

"No? Not in the boys' world? Where the men call the shots?"

"Not in *my* world," he said, defensively. "I'm not used to a woman being in charge."

"What are you used to?" I was thinking of the world I'd grown up in: men smoking out on the stoop and the women in the kitchen. Lace doilies on the backs of armchairs. Framed pictures of faraway places that nobody would ever visit on the walls.

He was the one to surprise me. He sat at my side on the sofa and pulled me over his lap. "I like to take the first step," he said. "Ask the girl out. Take her on a date. Bring her flowers. See if there's chemistry."

"Clearly, there's chemistry," I said to the sofa. "You tasted for yourself."

"But you're so forward," he said. "That can't go unpunished. I mean, I don't even know your name."

My pussy clenched. This wasn't how I'd envisioned the fantasy at all. I'd thought I would shock him, that he would appreciate a girl with a little spunk. But I hadn't expected this—his hand on my ass, delivering a blistering, over-the-knee spanking within moments of me entering his shop.

"Every time you walked past," he said, and he punctuated each word with a slap, "I thought of doing this. Your skirts are too short, do you know that?" He was tanning my hide with his big, strong palm and I couldn't respond. The way my clit felt bumping against his knee was sublime. But finally I managed, "Too short for what?"

"Too short for your own good," he said, and he pushed me from his lap so I was on the floor, looking at him. His erection was outlined beneath his slacks. I started to come forward, so I could undo his fly, release his cock. I wanted to suck him. I could practically feel his cockhead in my mouth. So I was shocked when he pushed me away.

"You know what you need?"

"Your cock."

He grimaced at me, and I said, "Oh, what? Girls in your world don't say the word *cock*? Or maybe they don't suck it. Wouldn't want to spoil their lip gloss."

"Behind the shed. I was right before. That's what you need. A long hard session with an old leather belt where nobody could hear you cry. Tune you up in no time."

"And then what?" I asked, though my pussy was responding to his words, juices dripping down my thighs. "Then I become one of those airheaded girls with the perfect flip? Someone you can control with a look?"

He shook his head. "I can't see you ever being under control," he said. "I'm sure you'd need a pretty steady diet of discipline."

Had I thought I was wet before? I was making a silky puddle between my legs. But I would not lose my moxie. "And you think you're the man for the job?"

"I'm dead sure of it," he said.

"But what about the girls you date? Those princesses."

"I have a theory about that," he said, and he stood and pulled me to standing, then led me toward the back of the shop. "You know what you can't do?"

I shook my head.

He stopped me in the hall, tilted my chin so I was looking into his eyes. "When I ask you a question, you answer."

"Yes," I said quickly.

"That's not how you answer."

"Yes, Tommy?" I tried, feeling less sure of myself now.

"Oh, so you're clever. You know my name, and I don't know yours."

"I'm Janie," I said. "Jane."

"All right, Janie." He looked stern, like I'd disappointed him. "You, with all your tricks, all your fancy plans. You don't even know what you need." He pushed me down then once more, so

I was on my knees gazing up at him. "When we're alone, like this. I'm going to be in charge. And you're going to do what I say. So you say, 'Yes, Sir' or 'No, Sir.' Shall we try again?"

"Yes, Sir," I said, and he continued down the hall with me following after in a crawl. When we'd reached the lounge in back, Tommy stood me up again. "The problem with princesses is that you can't fuck them the way you'd like to. You can't tie them up at night. Or use handcuffs. Or a butt plug. You can't spank them when they're naughty or flog them when they need it. You can't wash the bad words from their mouths with a bar of soap—because they never fucking say bad words."

He was stripping me as he spoke, and I saw that there was a basin of water back here and a stack of towels.

"So I've been thinking—as you have pranced by all spring in those too-short skirts of yours—that I don't need a princess."

And then he had me up on the table on my back and he was spreading thick lotion over my pussy using one of those sexy bristle brushes.

"What I need is a bad girl, like you."

He started to shave me. I closed my eyes. I was in heaven, the way he pinched my nether lips as he worked. The way he paid such careful attention to whisking away every last stray bit of hair. My fantasy had definitely come to life.

"Why do you think I'm a bad girl?" I panted.

"Because you're the exact opposite of every good girl I ever dated. You know, I came this close to getting married last fall." He kept working. I watched him as he focused on me.

"It was…" he said slowly, "a close shave."

I was surprised as he spoke, because I'd almost married a man who wanted a Barbie girl. I'd escaped. Like he had.

When he was done, he used a wet towel to rinse me, and then he used those fluffy towels to dry me off. He tested his work with his tongue, and I said, "If you keep doing that, Sir, I'm going to come." I thought it was the right thing to say.

"Fine," he said, looking up at me with his chin wet with my glossy juices. "And then I'll punish you."

My whole world seemed to freeze as he slid two fingers into my pussy.

"How? How will you...Sir?" I managed to tack on at the end.

"We'll start with my belt."

I sighed. I wanted to feel his belt. Desperately, I wanted to, but I couldn't help but ask, "Why?" I needed to hear the words.

"Why will I punish you? Because you're such a forward, pushy tart. Demanding that I take care of you. Not waiting for me to make the first move."

"You didn't. You never did." I didn't mean to sound accusatory. But I had waited. God, I had waited for months.

"I would have," he said. "I was biding my time."

"You were driving me fucking crazy." I didn't care that I'd forgotten the proper words. I was telling him the truth.

"Maybe that was part of my plan," he said, and then he refocused his attention on my split and I came in a flash; the way he made sweet circles over my clit was too dreamy.

In seconds, while I was still lost in that haze of bliss, he had me flipped and bent over the table. I heard the sound of his belt pulling free from the loops of his slacks, and I tensed my thighs in anticipation of the first blow. My ass was still warm from the hand spanking he'd delivered in the front room. I was pretty, pink and primed.

"What I need," he said, and he stung me with a fierce stroke from the start, "is a girl who can put on a princess act every once in a while so my family will get off my back. A girl who can stifle the four-letter words over a Sunday-night dinner. What do you think?"

"What do you mean, Sir?" I was having a hard time responding.

"Most people I know playact in the bedroom. They try to be all kinky when they're so fucking vanilla. I know who you are. I'm asking you to playact *out* of the bedroom. Pretend you're vanilla when we go have a dinner at my grandmother's house. But be the kinky fucking bad girl you are the rest of the time. Do you think you could do that?"

He was landing the blows steadily now, and I was moaning and writhing, my hips beating against the edge of the table.

"Can you do that, Janie?"

I sucked in my breath, because he'd dropped the belt, and I anticipated what was going to happen next. To my delight, I was right. He had unzipped his fly and he was pressing his cock against me.

"Yes," I said, to two things at once. "Yes, Sir," I said to his query and to his cock. "I can do that."

He was in me then, pushing forward so I felt his cock hammering all the way through me. I was so turned on I could hardly think. His cock was thick and hard and seemed to reach places inside me that hadn't been touched before. And all the time Tommy fucked me, he had his hand wrapped in my hair and he kept whispering the things he was going to do to me. The things he couldn't wait to do to me.

"Oh god," I whimpered. "Oh my fucking god."

"You know, I'll have to wash your mouth out when I get you home."

"Why, Sir?"

"Because you can't seem to go two seconds without saying the word 'fuck.'"

"No, Sir, I fucking can't," I said as he made me come a second time. Tommy slammed into me even faster after that, thrusting so hard he moved the table, and us with it, several feet forward. Then he pulled out and came all over my backside, rubbing his semen into my heated skin with the palm of his hand.

After, he washed me with a damp towel and dried me once more. Then he cleaned up the back room while I got dressed. I followed around after him, watching as he returned the shop to normal. The faded *Playboys* in their place. The blinds up.

"Let's go to my place," Tommy said.

"Yes, Sir," I said.

"That's right." He smiled. "Whenever we're with my family, you'll call me Tommy," he said as he led me to his car. "And you'll wear a decent-length skirt and a pair of panties. But don't worry, little girl, when I get you home after, I will take care of you. Exactly how you need."

He stopped at his car and lifted my skirt. He ran his palm over my mound and smiled.

"What do you think?" he asked. And I thought about everything I'd gone through to make it to this point. The waiting. The hoping. The near-disaster of an almost-tragic marriage. I'd survived a close shave, only to be given a kind I'd never truly believed possible.

"Yes, Sir," I said as I got into his car.

ABOUT THE AUTHORS

LAILA BLAKE (lailablake.com) is a bilingual German native with an MA in applied linguistics, working as a translator and English teacher in Cologne, Germany. With a special interest in human verbal and nonverbal communication, she spends her evenings and weekends penning character-driven romance and erotica for modern women.

HEIDI CHAMPA (heidichampa.blogspot.com) has been published in numerous anthologies including *Best Women's Erotica 2010, Playing with Fire, Irresistible* and *Best Erotic Romance 2013*. She has also steamed up the pages of *Bust* Magazine. If you prefer your erotica in electronic form, she can be found at Clean Sheets, Ravenous Romance, Oysters & Chocolate and The Erotic Woman.

ANDREA DALE (AndreaDaleAuthor.com) has been called a "legendary erotica heavy-hitter" by the über-legendary Violet

Blue. Her work has appeared in 20 year's best volumes as well as about 100 other anthologies. She no longer has a pool, much less a pool girl...but she often fantasizes about both.

JEREMY EDWARDS (jeremyedwardserotica.com) is the author of *Rock My Socks Off*, *Spark My Moment* and most recently *The Pleasure Dial: An Erotocomedic Novel of Old-Time Radio*. His libidinous tales have appeared in over fifty anthologies, including The Mammoth Book of Best New Erotica series.

A. M. HARTNETT (amhartnett.com) published her first erotic short in 2006. Since then, she has been featured in several anthologies, including Cleis's *Going Down*, *Sudden Sex* and *Best Erotic Romance 2013*.

TILLY HUNTER (tillyhunter.co.uk) is a British author and newspaper journalist with a wicked imagination and a fondness for stories of good food, wholesome living and BDSM. Her work has been published by Xcite Books, House of Erotica, MLR Press and the websites Every Night Erotica and Oysters & Chocolate.

CRYSTAL JORDAN is originally from California, but has lived all over the United States. Currently, she serves as a librarian at a university in her home state, and she writes paranormal, contemporary, futuristic and erotic romance. She has published stories with Kensington Aphrodisia, Harlequin Spice Briefs, Ellora's Cave, Cleis Press and Samhain Publishing.

SOMMER MARSDEN (sommermarsden.blogspot.com) has been called "One of the top storytellers in the erotica genre" by Violet Blue. Her erotic novels include *Restless Spirit, Boys Next*

Door and *Learning to Drown*. The wine-swigging, dachshund-owning author's work runs the gamut from bondage to zombies. Current addictions include insane workouts and buying (too many) T-shirts.

DELILAH NIGHT (delilahnight.com) is an American living in Singapore with her husband and young children. With unlimited time and money, she would become either a sexologist or a pastry chef.

KATHRYN O'HALLORAN (kathrynohalloran.blogspot.com) was told to write what she knows; despite that, she now writes erotica. She finds the research grueling but she goes at it with guts and determination. She has recently released her debut novel, *The Bad Girls' Club*.

Award-winning author **KATE PEARCE** was born into a large family of girls in England, and spent much of her childhood living very happily in a dream world. Kate is also published by Signet Eclipse, Kensington Aphrodisia, Carina Press, Ellora's Cave, Cleis Press and Virgin Black Lace/Cheek.

DEVIN PHILLIPS only recently started writing naughty stories at a kinky boyfriend's request. The boyfriend went away, but she's addicted. Her stories have appeared in the anthologies *Occupied*, *Frequent Flyers*, *Double Birdie* and *Swings Both Ways*.

GISELLE RENARDE is a queer Canadian, avid volunteer, contributor to more than one hundred short-story anthologies and author of numerous electronic and print books, including *Anonymous*, *Nanny State* and *My Mistress' Thighs*. Ms. Renarde lives across from a park with two bilingual cats who sleep on her head.

ELISA SHARONE's (elisasharone.tumblr.com) heretofore super-secret sex writing has soaked hundreds of thousands of panties across the globe. She's wandering a new path, dipping into the deepest, darkest recesses of her imagination to bring readers brain-melting erotica that leaves them gasping for more.

SOPHIA VALENTI (sophiavalenti.blogspot.com) is the author of *Indecent Desires*, an erotic novella of spanking and submission. Her fiction has appeared in the Harlequin Spice anthologies *Alison's Wonderland* and *With This Ring, I Thee Bed*, as well as several Pretty Things Press books, including *Kiss My Ass*, *Skirting the Issue*, *Smart Ass* and *Torn*.

Gifted with a salacious imagination, **SASHA WHITE's** brand of *Romance with Heat, and Erotica with Heart* is all about sassy women and sexy men. With over thirty stories published by Berkley, Kensington, Samhain, Black Lace and Cleis Press, this Canadian author has become a reader favorite.

CORA ZANE (corazane.com) lives in an area of northern Louisiana known as "out in the sticks." She is the author of *What She Doesn't Know*, *Wicked Obsession* and the Werekind Were-wolf series of erotic romance e-books. She has also published work in several anthologies, including *Morning, Noon and Night*; *Coming Together: Hungry for Love* and *Dirtyville*.

ABOUT
THE EDITOR

Called "a trollop with a laptop" by *East Bay Express,* "a literary siren" by Good Vibrations and "the mistress of literary erotica" by Violet Blue, **ALISON TYLER** is naughty and she knows it.

Over the past two decades, Ms. Tyler has written more than twenty-five explicit novels, including *Tiffany Twisted, Melt with You* and *The ESP Affair.* Her novels and short stories have been translated into Japanese, Dutch, German, Italian, Norwegian, Spanish and Greek. When not writing sultry short stories, she edits erotic anthologies, including *Alison's Wonderland, Kiss My Ass, Skirting the Issue* and *Torn.* She is also the author of several novellas including *Cuffing Kate, Giving In* and *A Taste of Chi.*

Ms. Tyler is loyal to coffee (black), lipstick (red), and tequila (straight). She has tattoos, but no piercings; a wicked tongue, but a quick smile; and bittersweet memories, but no regrets. She believes it won't rain if she doesn't bring an umbrella, prefers hot and dry to cold and wet, and loves to spout her favorite motto:

You can sleep when you're dead. She chooses Led Zeppelin over the Beatles, the Cure over NIN and the Stones over everyone. Yet although she appreciates good rock, she has a pitiful weakness for '80s hair bands.

She has worked as a popcorn girl, maid, personal assistant, salesclerk, page editor, ghostwriter, and receptionist. But she's most proud of rewriting the *Kama Sutra*.

In all things important, she remains faithful to her partner of eighteen years, but she still can't choose just one perfume.

More from Alison Tyler

Frenzy
60 Stories of Sudden Sex
Edited by Alison Tyler

"Toss out the roses and box of candies. This isn't a prolonged seduction. This is slammed against the wall in an alleyway sex, and it's all that much hotter for it."
—Erotica Readers & Writers Association
ISBN 978-1-57344-331-9 $14.95

Best Bondage Erotica
Edited by Alison Tyler

Always playful and dangerously explicit, these arresting fantasies grab you, tie you down, and never let you go.
ISBN 978-1-57344-173-5 $15.95

Afternoon Delight
Erotica for Couples
Edited by Alison Tyler

"Alison Tyler evokes a world of heady sensuality where fantasies are fearlessly explored and dreams gloriously realized."
—Barbara Pizio, Executive Editor,
Penthouse Variations
ISBN 978-1-57344-341-8 $14.95

Got a Minute?
60 Second Erotica
Edited by Alison Tyler

"Classy but very, very dirty, this is one of the few very truly indispensable filth anthologies around." —*UK Forum*
ISBN 978-1-57344-404-0 $14.95

Playing with Fire
Taboo Erotica
Edited by Alison Tyler

"Alison Tyler has managed to find the best stories from the best authors, and create a book of fantasies that—if you're lucky enough, or determined enough—just might come true." —Clean Sheets
ISBN 978-1-57344-348-7 $14.95

Ordering is easy! Call us toll free or fax us to place your MC/VISA order.
You can also mail the order form below with payment to:
Cleis Press, 2246 Sixth St., Berkeley, CA 94710.

ORDER FORM

QTY	TITLE	PRICE

Ad
book

nal
dents